BORN A RAMBLIN' MAN

"Michel Lee Garrett writes tense stories full of humanity and grit. ***Born a Ramblin' Man*** is a master class in writing crime fiction."
—**John C. Foster**, author of ***The Hard Six***

"***Born a Ramblin' Man*** marks the debut collection of a ferocious and talented writer. Michel Lee Garrett brings to her work in equal measures a vivid eye for character, a whip-lash storytelling sensibility, and an unquenchable thirst for justice. Haunted characters and haunted lives roam these pages, each one with Michel's unmistakable touch. This is one not to be missed."
—**James D.F. Hannah**, Shamus Award-winning author of ***Behind the Wall of Sleep*** and ***Because the Night***

"14 engaging tales of drifters and grifters, con artists and conned, has-beens and never-weres – Michel Lee Garrett is the perfect guide for a gripping trip you don't want to miss. Ramble on!"
— **Gregory Galloway**, award-winning author of ***All We Trust*** and ***Just Thieves***

"Good God! Michel's instantly iconic hero Ray is the dusty soul of America: a hunter, a detective, and even a prophet, one who proves God exists in his distant heaven but the devil's waiting at the crossroads—and much more fun. With a Willie Nelson t-shirt, cowboy boots and a joint hanging off his lip, he's on the search for truth in stories that flawlessly join old detective noir with country charm. Michel Lee Garrett is one of America's up-and-coming great storytellers, and if you love compelling detective yarns or just some old-fashioned crime stories, you have to read ***Born a Ramblin' Man***."
—**T. Fox Dunham**, author of ***The Street Martyr*** and ***Mercy***

BORN A RAMBLIN' MAN

FOURTEEN TALES OF THIEVES, KILLERS, VAGABONDS, AND LOST SOULS

MICHEL LEE GARRETT

Published by Shotgun Honey Books

215 Loma Road
Charleston, WV 25314
www.ShotgunHoney.com

Cover Art, "Ramblin' Man," by Mary Siniscalchi.
Cover Design by Bad Fido.

ISBN-10: 1-956957-80-4
ISBN-13: 978-1-956957-80-8

10 9 8 7 6 5 4 3 2 1   25 24 23 22 21 20 19

STORIES

BORN A
RAMBLIN' MAN

BORN A RAMBLIN' MAN

The summer of his squandered youth after he left the Navy, Raymond Reynolds found himself leaving out of Nashville, Tennessee and wondering if he should head on down to New Orleans.

It was one night on this southward ramble, passing through some nameless patch of country lost to time, that Ray stumbled into a vagrant's oasis: a roadside plaza boasting diesel pumps, a liquor store, a slasher flick motel, and a so-called gentlemen's club named Filthy Billy's. He didn't care to find out how accurate that name was.

Instead, he wasted the last of his cash on a bottom-shelf bottle of something brown and sat behind a dumpster waiting for a southbound tractor trailer. Until then, he was content to drink and pluck away at his guitar, his lone souvenir from his misadventures in Nashville — one that he had, um, "liberated," Ray might've described it, from its previous owners.

He was liver-deep into his bottle when a southbound big rig finally rumbled into the empty lot. He quieted his guitar. A driver emerged and stood smoking, an ogre's frame silhouetted by brake lights. Ray expected him to head to the strip club, but instead he lit a second cigarette and continued waiting in the darkness.

Before long, a second truck pulled in off the highway, circled the lot, and parked beside the first. The ogre opened his trailer. A new figure, tall and narrow like a dead tree, exited the second rig. They stood conspiring. Ray pushed back the wide brim of his flat-top Stetson hat and began creeping forward through the shadows. Snatches of conversation reached his ears.

"That ain't what we agreed," the ogre rumbled.

"Ain't no different," croaked the narrow man. "Hell, it ain't even that far."

Ray sidled the length of the trailer and knelt behind the open doors, waiting for his moment.

"It ain't about how far. It's about risk and reward."

"It's good money, and they're already packaged for transport. No trouble for you at all. Just a point A and a point B that needs gettin' to, and you know he don't like to be kept waiting."

Ray peered around the doors. The two men turned their backs and approached the second truck. *Here goes!* The rambler clambered like a rat up into the belly of the trailer. Several dozen boxes of fireworks filled the inside. He curled up behind a stack of red, white, and blue bottle rockets. *Goddamn, is it really almost the Fourth of July?* And then a second question: *How long has it been since I been home…?*

Ray swayed where he sat for a long time, but the ogre did not return. Before he knew it, he'd slipped into a drunken sleep. He dreamt of burgers grilling over open flames, drooling on the trailer floor.

When he woke, it was to the sound of a woman screaming.

Ray jolted upright, face slathered in saliva, still half drunk, and the other half already hung over. He poked his head out from behind his rockets.

His blood chilled in his veins.

Two young women were locked in a cage inside the trailer. One couldn't be more than sixteen, wearing a Nashville Christian School uniform, unconscious on the floor. The other was older only by a couple years, hard-eyed and dressed in denim and leather, shaking her cage bars and screaming herself raw.

"Anyone! Help! *Hellp!* Get us the fuck out of here!"

Goddammit. Ray sucked his teeth. *Should've picked a different truck...*

The girl continued screaming. The truck lurched suddenly to the right, throwing Ray off balance, then braked hard, sending boxes tumbling down. Ray found himself buried in fireworks, groaning. The girl's screaming hushed.

"Wait. Is someone...?"

Ray held his tongue. The ogre ripped the trailer doors open — three hundred pounds of hulking muscle in overalls, roaring with fury. The girl turned to him, hellfire in her eyes.

"You! Piece of shit!" she shrieked. "Make you feel big and strong, kidnappin' little girls? If there's *anyone here,* if *anyone* can hear me, please—"

The ogre unlocked the cage and threw her to the floor. "Shut your fucking mouth!" He drove a boot into her stomach. "No trouble, he promised me! Twelve hours you were supposed to be under! And here you are, screaming like a goddamn banshee!"

Slapping and yelping filled the trailer. Ray winced.

"You don't understand," the girl spat blood. "I'll *kill* you, you motherfu—"

The driver pulled a Smith & Wesson from his overalls and pressed the barrel to her temple. "No, sweetheart. *You* don't understand. I'll kill *you,* I swear to *god,* if you dare open your mouth *one more fuckin' time.* You understand?"

The girl didn't answer, staring up at him through newly blackened eyes. He moved his finger to the trigger.

"I said, you *understand*?"

"Yeah," she seethed. "I understand."

"Then keep your dickhole closed 'till someone pays for you to open it." He shoved her back into the cage. "Next time I have to come back here," he said, relocking it, "I'm putting a bullet between your pretty eyes."

The ogre thundered out, slamming the trailer closed. In the

reformed darkness, the girl's rage melted into tears. Ray sat there, buried in boxes with his pounding head, wondering what to do. The girl caught her sobs in her throat and forced them back down.

"I know you're here," she said, sniffing back tears. "I heard you."

Ray bit his lip. Could've been the engine groaning, right? Maybe he could just keep his mouth shut, stay hidden, and take the first chance to slip away.

"Nothing?" she said. "Just gonna sit here, ignoring this? Or..." Her tone sharpened. "You with *them*? Supposed to keep an eye on us, make sure we can't get out?"

Again Ray said nothing, part of him *still* wondering if he could get away with hiding quietly — a vagabond Jonah, ignoring the storm raging around the ship he'd stowed away aboard. He thought about something his dad used to tell him.

"All you ever do is make *one* decision in life, over and over," the old man said. "Just the one. Ain't sayin' I always made it right. Far from it. But everything you do, you can choose to help folks, or to not. The rest is jus' details."

And the devil, as they say, truly is in the details, ain't he?

Laughter punctured his silence. "Okay, wait," she said, "I get it now. You just wanna hang out and *watch*, right? This how you get your kicks, you disgusting animal? You gutless pervert? *You sick fuck?*"

"Woahwoahwoah, that ain't fair," Ray finally protested. "Y-You're making all sorts of assumptions, and..."

"*A'int fair?!* Listen shitheel, all I know is I got promised good money dancing at Filthy Billy's, and next thing I know I'm locked in a cage being fuckin' *kidnapped*, and you think *you're* bein' treated unfairly?"

"...Fair 'nuff."

"So?"

"So...?"

"*Who the fuck are you?* Why are you here?"

"Oh, I'm just, uh… a ramblin' man, y'know? All I wanted was a free ride."

"You, me, and everybody else. How'd that turn out for ya?"

"Well, I'm *here*."

"Wouldya look at that, me too. Lemme guess: now you're thinkin' you *clearly* made a big mistake and want off this truck, *asap*, am I right?"

"Hey, I'm not a sap!"

"My god. Listen. Dumbass? Are you gonna help me outta here, please? Like… now?"

One choice. That's really all you get in life? Ray sighed. *Might as well make it better than the old man did.*

"Yeah, I reckon my dumb ass is gonna try. Pretty sure I'm about the last person you want in your corner."

"You're higher on my list than our chauffeur. What's your name?"

"Ray."

"Joan, charmed, I'm sure — you know how to pick a lock?"

"Oh sure," he grumbled, emerging from beneath his fireworks. "No 'nice to meet ya, Ray,' nothin' like that?"

"It ain't 'nice to meet ya!' This is all *terrible*! How goddamn dumb *are* you?"

"Um… fairly."

In spite of herself, she chuckled. "Least you realize it."

"The only one more dangerous than the fool who don't realize it," Ray stumbled toward her, "is the fool who do."

"And which are you?"

"…wha?"

She sighed. "Nevermind. Just get me out."

Ray knelt in front of the cage, trying to eyeball the mechanisms inside the lock. He produced his old swiss army knife and lighter, then struck the flame to better inspect the lock.

"The fuck are you *doing*?" Joan yelled.

"Keep your voice down! I'm *trying* to get you out?"

"The light! The fireworks everywhere!"

"I'm serious, if Shrek comes back here again there is *nothing* I can do, so *shut*, please, the fuck, *up!*"

Which was the exact moment the other victim in the cage roused blearily back to consciousness, briefly processed her surroundings, and immediately began screaming in blood-curdling terror.

"No, no, no! Fuck! Shhhh!" Ray tried his best to look reassuring. "I'm here to help you get out! Everything's fine!"

Joan bypassed Ray's attempts at subtlety, gagging the younger girl from behind.

"Listen now," she snapped. "I already tried screaming. It ain't gonna work. If the bastard drivin' hears you, he's gonna come back here 'n' kill us both."

Tears welled in the teenager's hazel eyes.

"Hey now," Joan continued. "Listen! It ain't all bad. We're gettin' out of this. Way I see it, we got the upper hand here. You and I ain't even supposed to be *awake* yet, and we got a secret weapon — Mr. Stowaway here, who the driver knows nothin' about."

"And I, just to be clear," Ray offered, "am definitely not some pervert who's only here because he likes to watch, okay?"

The girl made muffled noises of protest, her terror renewed.

Joan looked at Ray like he was an idiot. "Why would you say that?"

"'Cause it's… true…?"

"When you say it like that, it sounds like you *definitely are*."

"Wha!? But you had said!? And I didn't want her to think—"

The younger girl resumed sobbing.

"Please," she moaned. "I'll be quiet…"

Joan sighed and released her. She curled into a ball and sobbed softly into her knees. Joan and Ray both looked to each other. He pointed to her. She pointed to him. Ray turned back to the younger girl, frowning doubtfully.

"So, uh," he ventured, "what's your name?"

Sobbing was the only answer.

"I'm Ray. That's Joan."

Still, nothing returned but crying.

"She was right," he continued. "We're gettin' out of this. You'll be safe 'n' sound in your own bed 'fore you know it."

The sobbing continued.

Ray sighed. "Look, I ain't good at bein' comforting, okay? One time, had this girlfriend Owen, right? And her cat, Mr. Socks, he was all black with white feet, looked like he was wearing socks, got out and ran away. And *my* dumb ass tells her at least she don't have to scoop up cat shit and clean up hairballs no more. *Not* the right answer, turns out."

"Did…" The girl's voice sounded like it might break at any moment. "Did she find him?"

Ray blinked. "Yep," he lied. "Came back the next day. Safe 'n' sound."

Joan laughed. Ray glared at her.

The younger girl smiled. Her breathing steadied and slowed. "Mr. Socks," she laughed. "It's a cute name."

"What's yours?"

"Kayleigh," she said.

"Great, we all know each other," snapped Joan. "Now how're we goin' to get out?"

"I *was* gonna pick your lock," Ray said, "but *someone* started hollerin' at me."

Joan stuck her hand through the bars. "Give it here."

"Wha?"

"The knife! I'll pick it my damn self," she grumbled. "What kind of thief cain't pick a lock by feel?"

Ray handed it over. She worked one of the attachments into the lock, digging like a miner searching for gold.

"Never said I was a *thief*, by the way. Said I was a *rambler*."

"Never met one who wasn't the other."

"Pleased to meet you?"

"Oh yeah?" She pointed to his guitar — rich mahogany, the neck inlaid with silver roses for fret markers, and the pickguard adorned with an image of sunrise breaking over a mountain ridge. "Pretty nice guitar. Where'd you buy it?"

"Um… okay, thing about *that*, is…"

"Exactly. What I thought."

"Wait! This might sound crazy, but does it *really* count as 'stealing' if it's from the *goddamn Nashville Mafia*? Right? There's gotta be, like, a Robin Hood rule or something…"

"You're *so* full of shit," Joan laughed.

"I'm serious!"

"*Suuuuure.*" Components clicked inside the lock. She pushed the door open. "You're a regular criminal fuckin' mastermind. Just look how quick you got that lock open!"

Ray pouted while Joan exited the cage. Kayleigh stayed behind, kneeling with her eyes closed.

"…and even though I walk through the shadow of the valley of death, I shall fear no evil…"

Ray looked to Joan, who looked back to him. Ray pointed to himself, then to Joan, then finally to Kayleigh. Joan sighed and rolled her eyes.

"Hey dummy," she said.

Ray regretted letting her handle it.

Kayleigh looked up to Joan with trembling eyes.

"Prayer ain't gonna help you now."

She gasped. "How could you say that? It was General Robert E. Lee who said prayer is our most *powerful* weapon!"

"Probably why he lost."

"What I think she's *trying* to say," Ray intervened, "i-i-is, um, like the Bible says? God helps those who help *themselves*. And we need to get to helpin' ourselves offa this truck, 'cause we ain't got much time."

Joan scowled. "How you figure?"

"Feller the driver was talkin' to said he didn't have far to go."

"Wait y'all," said Kayleigh.

"Ain't no time for fuckin' prayer!" snapped Joan.

"No, don't you hear? It's… quieter."

The steady whine of the wheels had softened. The truck had slowed, and the hum of the highway had been replaced by the crunching of gravel.

Joan grimaced. "Shit."

"What?"

"We're nearly there."

Kayleigh gasped, gazing upward. "Your rod and your staff! They comfort me!"

"Ain't no time for—"

"You prepare a table before me in the presence of my enemies!"

"Nevermind. What about you, Robin Hood? You got a plan?"

Ray bit his lip, furiously searching for a way out and fidgeting with his lighter. *Wait.* He looked at the lighter, then to the closest box of bottle rockets.

"Fuckin' *duh*," Ray said. "The rockets!"

"You realize they got guns?"

"Said yourself, we got the element of surprise!"

"Think that's enough?"

"It ain't all," Kayleigh said, stepping up beside them. "We also have—"

Joan cut her off. "Are you about to say prayer?"

Kayleigh blushed. "N-No."

"No?"

"I was gonna say *faith*, actually…"

"Hell, I'll take faith," Ray said. "If you got any this might work, hold onto it. We're gonna need it."

The truck shuddered to a stop.

"Wherever they was takin' us…" Joan said.

"We're here." Ray took a deep breath. "Back behind the boxes, grab some'a the rockets, let's *go*…"

They waited, breath baited, for their captors to come.

Joan's knee bounced like a rubber ball. "Hey," she turned to Kayleigh, "now don't you say a goddamn word, but, um…" Her voice softened. "Maybe finish that prayer you were saying?"

Kayleigh smiled and placed her hand on Joan's anxious knee. Joan placed her own hand overtop. "Even though I walk through the valley of the shadow of death, I will fear no evil," Kayleigh whispered. Joan bowed her head.

Ray had never been a praying man. He removed his hat anyway.

"For you are with me — your rod and your staff, they comfort me..."

A door slammed closed. Muffled voices murmured outside.

"You prepare a table for me in the presence of my enemies. You anoint my head with oil, and my cup overfloweth..."

Footsteps approached. The voices had reached outside the trailer doors.

"Surely goodness and mercy will follow me all the days of my life," Kayleigh prayed. "And I will dwell in the house of the Lord forever. Amen."

"Amen," Joan said.

"Amen," Ray mumbled.

The handles turned and the trailer doors opened. The ogre entered, joined by a new figure in a tailored suit, designer shades and Rolex watch.

"Bit of a spitfire," the ogre was saying. "Might have to remind her of her manners."

The buyer smiled. "I don't mind breaking 'em in. Part of the fun."

Ray, Joan and Kayleigh each readied their bottle rockets, taking aim. Ray flicked his lighter. It didn't catch.

"Part of *your* fun, maybe," the ogre said. "Made *my* job more difficult. About an extra fifteen percent's worth, I'd say."

"Wait a minute." The buyer moved his sunglasses down, revealing bloodshot blue eyes. "Where the fuck are they?"

"Where..." The ogre turned to the cage, and grew fury-red in the face. "Those fucking cunts!"

Ray thought they were out of time, but the buyer bought them another couple seconds. From inside his jacket, he produced a pearl-handled 9mm H&K and pointed it at the ogre's chest. Ray flicked the lighter again. Still nothing.

"I don't take kindly to bein' fucked with!"

"I ain't fuckin' with you!"

"Then *where* is my *goddamn merchandise?!*"

Joan leaned into Ray's ear. "So," she whispered, "you gonna get it up?"

"I swear," desperately flicking, "this has never happened to me before…"

The lighter finally sparked to life.

"There's no way they got off," the driver said. "They're still in here!"

The ogre began fe-fi-fo-fumming his way toward the back of the trailer. Ray brought the flame from fuse to fuse with shaking hands. The wires glowed red as the fire ate its way toward the rockets.

"When I find you," roared the ogre, "I'm gonna—"

"Wait a second," said the buyer. "You hear that?"

The driver stopped, mere feet away. The hissing of fuses filled the quiet truck. The ogre swallowed hard.

"Get back! They—"

Light, sound, and color screamed through the truck as the rockets burst to life, sparks and fire following like comet tails. One surged right into the ogre's sternum, where it burst like a grenade. The beast stumbled backwards, beard burning.

Ray dropped his lighter and led the charge: "Thundercats *hoooo!*"

He grabbed Kayleigh's wrist with one hand and his guitar with the other, charging forward into the chaos. Rockets whistling and popping around him, he brought his boot up into the ogre's crotch, hard enough to send him to the floor. But between them and freedom still stood the buyer. Imposingly tall, head shaved to a polished dome, beard trimmed to cling to his jawline — and pointing his pistol squarely at Ray's chest.

"You got something of mine," he said, gesturing to Kayleigh. "Ain't no one ever told you stealing was wrong?"

Ray didn't answer. Kayleigh's grip tightened around his hand.

"Tell you what. I'm a generous man. You hand her over, and I won't put a hole through your belly." He laughed — a sound like cars crashing. "I'd call that a pretty good deal. Better than you deserve."

Ray gulped, hoping for a miracle. *Wait a second… Where's Joan?*

He glanced back just in time to see her, still at the rear of the truck, lighting another rocket. Ray ducked, yanking Kayleigh down with him.

The rocket ignited and whistled over their heads, burning forward toward the buyer's face. The reflection in his glasses grew brighter, his eyes widening behind their lenses. "Oh *shi-*" It exploded inches from his nose, leaving him screaming on the floor and clutching his hands to his face.

"Jesus Christ, I'm fucking blind!"

Ray put his boot over the buyer's wrist and yanked away his gun. "I'd call that a pretty good deal," he said. "Better than you deserve."

"I'll kill you…!" He swung at Ray, in the wrong direction.

Ray left him there, still screaming, and jumped from the trailer. They were in some warehouse, rusted machinery lining sheet metal walls. Joan ran to catch up, quieting the buyer with a hard kick to the temple. She jumped down beside Ray but Kayleigh lingered inside, still kneeling with her head bowed over the blind man.

"Ain't no time for…!" But Joan's words caught in her throat as Kayleigh turned back to them, shaking the buyer's car keys.

"Thought we'd need a ride out of here," she said, climbing down.

"Thought the Bible said something about not stealing," Ray said.

Kayleigh blushed. "M-Men do not despise a thief if he steals to satisfy his hunger when he's starving!"

Joan nodded. "Proverbs 6:30."

The younger girl gasped. "How did…?"

Joan took the stolen keys. "Maybe we're more alike than either of us would like to admit."

"Hey!" Ray pointed to a luxury SUV parked at the other end of the warehouse. "Maybe we should make like a banana and, uh, *get the fuck outta here*?"

They sprinted toward their escape vehicle. The ogre, his beard singed off and blistered chest flesh visible behind his charred overalls, stumbled out of the truck. He raised his handgun, firing wildly. The SUV's back window imploded, showering them with broken glass as they piled inside.

"Hit it!" Ray hollered, watching the ogre take closer aim.

Joan cranked the keys and slammed the gas. Gunfire screamed, taking out the passenger-side mirror as their tires squealed against the warehouse floor. Bullets flying past them, they sped through the open warehouse doors.

Only minutes later, they were back on the highway, the entire ordeal behind them. Ray looked down at the pearl-handled pistol in his hand, wondering if he could pawn it for liquor money. Instead, he wiped away his prints, rolled down the window, and flung it into the underbrush.

"Thank you God," Kayleigh said, eyes closed and hands clasped, "for—"

A terrific explosion interrupted her, shaking the earth beneath their tires. In their rearview mirror, a volcano of fireworks erupted. Each of them looked at the others.

No one said anything.

Kayleigh cleared her throat.

"Thank you God, who are so good and merciful, for your protection and your guidance today…"

Joan rolled her eyes, but with a small smile. She turned to Ray. "So what's next?"

"You can let me off anywhere," he shrugged. "I ain't picky."

"What?"

"I prefer if you'd *stop*, but I can always tuck and roll…"

"No, you idiot, I—"

Kayleigh stopped praying. "You're… leaving? Just like that?"

Ray looked back and forth between them. Kayleigh stared at him, earnest and expectant. Joan had turned away, watching the road with a sour scowl.

"Well… yeah? I mean, what else would we even…?"

"I don't kn… I just…." Kayleigh sniffled. "Figured we'd at least find a police station, that you'd stick around until my parents came?"

"Yeah… no. I don't really *do* cops." Ray's cheeks burned. "I just…" He sighed. "I'm just doing what I do, okay?"

"What's that?" Kayleigh asked.

"*Leaving*," Joan spat.

"Well… it's time," Ray shrugged. "I hope you'll understand."

The look on Kayleigh's face assured him that she did not. Tears rolled down her cheeks. Joan rested her hand on Kayleigh's, still not looking at Ray.

"I'll pray for you," Kayleigh said.

"I won't," Joan said.

Ray chuckled. "I wouldn't either."

Joan pulled over, but didn't bother to stop. Ray opened his door and looked back to them, tried to think of something to say, couldn't, then jumped without saying goodbye.

He fucked up the roll, landed hard, and stood up holding a throbbing shoulder. The SUV vanished into the horizon like the sun into the ocean. A nameless sadness burned deep inside his gut.

"Wait! Fuck!"

He'd forgotten his guitar in the backseat.

NEVER TAKE THE FIRST OFFER

Cera Dieben spent the summer after her sophomore year out in Vegas, living off the pocket cash of drunken tourists. Her friend Lucy had dropped out of their economics program at UCLA to become a call girl. She didn't mind Cera crashing on her couch, but cautioned her against picking pockets too carelessly.

"You never know whose pocket you're gonna reach into in this town," Lucy said.

Cera rolled her hazel eyes. Lucy visited strangers' hotel rooms for a living. Cera never moralized to her about the dangers of *that*. Now she was going to give lectures about the dangers of *Cera*'s livelihood?

She could take care of herself. Been doing it since she was sixteen.

"You don't need to worry about me," she said.

One blistering morning, Cera spied an easy mark. Tailored slacks, designer shades, tie undone. She read him as some self-important executive, intoxicated by the city of excess. Her bread and butter.

She fell in line behind him. As the Bellagio exhaled a torrent of tourists, she made her move. A casual brush against him as the traffic passed by, and his wallet and cellphone made their way from his pockets to hers. He stumbled on, none the wiser.

In the bathroom of a cantina around the corner, she checked the wallet. It contained three thousand dollars cash, in crisp hundred dollar bills. She whistled to herself, then made her way to the bar and ordered their most expensive tequila. When the bartender asked if she was old enough, she slipped a Benjamin into the tip jar.

He poured the tequila.

Sipping the sultry liquid, she inspected the phone. It was a new, allegedly smarter model, requiring a geometric pattern to open. Tipping the screen to the light, she identified a long smudge that snaked around the screen. She figured out the pattern by her third attempt.

The contents bored her. All his texts and emails were spreadsheets, numbers, financial reports, market analysis… blah, blah, blah. The same boring shit she waded through at her internship with a labor forecasting firm off the strip, when she even bothered to show up. She'd been hoping for explicit texts with a mistress or compromising photos. Something fun. She nearly pitched the thing, but some burgeoning instinct stopped her. She took a second pass over the numbers.

It took her another $80 glass of tequila, but Cera cracked it. The phone's owner, Duane Braddock, according to his email signature, was double-dealing. She was sure of it. Whatever he was involved in, he was reporting out two sets of numbers. One to someone named Elmore, and one to someone named Vinny. Something about short selling stock in advance of some big market shakeup in two weeks. There were promises of big money. Millions of dollars, big money. Legality didn't seem to be a concern.

It was basically the same model Vegas operated on, Cera mused — betting against the little guy, then raking in the dough when they went belly up.

Either Elmore or Vinny were going to make out like bandits, depending on which one was getting the real numbers. The other was screwed. Either way, Duane clearly planned to emerge on the winning side. Cera, ever the opportunist, wondered if she could find a way to wring any cash for herself out of this situation.

She pocketed the phone, ordered a tequila to go, and returned to Lucy's place to pull together a plan. Her friend's silver stilettos were gone from beside the door, a sure sign she was out with a client. Perfect. Problem was, a six pack of beer and American Idol distracted Cera almost immediately, and before long she was passed out and drooling on the couch cushions.

Then she awoke to Lucy's door getting kicked in.

Before she knew what was happening, she found herself pinned to the wall by her throat by some bald, muscle-bound brute with bulging veins. Behind him stood a thin figure with dark brows in a sharp black suit and emerald tie. Neither one was Duane Braddock. Cera groaned, still a little drunk. She picked the brute's pockets while she dangled.

"You're the one who met our friend Duane today, huh?" said the thin one. "Good thing he keeps his GPS turned on."

That one was the leader. Cera gasped and gargled. The thin one nodded to the brute. He released her throat, letting her fall to the floor.

"So," Cera gasped in between breaths, "are you Elmore or Vinny?"

The intruders glanced at each other. "We're asking the questions here," said the thin one.

Cera held up the business card she'd pulled from the brute's pocket. "James Rodrick, head of security, Elmore Industries," she read. Cera pointed to the thin man. "So that makes you Elmore."

The brute hoisted her by the throat again.

"You stole from my associate," Elmore said. "Unwise."

"At least... *I*... don't work... with *rats*," Cera choked out, the brute's fist tight around her windpipe.

Elmore paused. Cera had an opening.

"Duane! He's... playing... you!" Her face was turning blue. "Bet you already... suspected... didn't you?"

For a brief moment, a shadow of unease broke Elmore's composed exterior. It quickly returned, but Cera had already seen behind the mask.

"Put her down," Elmore said.

The brute complied. Cera crumpled, wheezing.

"You better start talking," Elmore said. "And start talking fast."

"That big deal going down in two weeks? Duane's been cooking the books. Two sets of numbers — one for you, and one for the guy he's double-crossing you for."

"Bullshit, boss. There's no way," brayed the brute. "You're gonna believe her?"

"Shaddup!" snapped Elmore. "You fuckin' galoot. Let her talk."

He listened, but he didn't look happy about it.

Cera couldn't help throwing salt in the wound. "Come on Mugsy, rub your two brain cells together. If you two are here 'cause Duane got robbed, where is *Duane*?"

"Out to dinner with his cousin Vincent," the brute answered. "Family's important."

"His cousin *Vinny*?"

Elmore cursed and kicked Lucy's furniture, beginning to see the full picture.

"See Mugsy? Bugsy gets it." Cera put on her best saleswoman smile. "Tell you what, for five thousand bucks, I'll give you the proof you need to confront him."

Elmore shook his head. "Counteroffer. How about I *don't* have Rodrick here break your neck, and you hand over whatever you got for free?"

Not getting her neck broken was a pretty good deal. But Cera never took the first offer — from *anyone* — regardless of what it was, and she never walked away unless somebody else was walking away with less. A woman has to have her principles.

"Only if you let me keep the cash from Mugsy's wallet," she said.

Rodrick opened his now-empty wallet. "Boss, I had five hundred bucks in here!"

"Shuddup, Mugsy." Elmore smiled at Cera, revealing perfect, pearly teeth. "Fine. Keep the money. But hand over the proof."

Cera chuckled, pulling out Duane's phone. She opened it to his last email to Vinny, which detailed the latest set of numbers and expected profits, and tossed it up to Elmore. His face darkened as he read the report.

"Looks like we need to have ourselves a 'Come to Jesus' meeting with Duane," he muttered.

Mugsy cracked his knuckles. "Does that mean we're done here?"

"Yeah. We're done here." He slipped the phone into his breast pocket. He looked briefly to Cera, still on the floor, then turned back to his muscle. "Take care of her. Make it quick."

Like a winning streak demolished by a losing hand, Cera's tenuous grasp on the situation vanished. Cold sweat ran down her neck.

A cruel smile twisted the brute's face.

"W-wait!" Cera had nowhere to go. For once, she couldn't think of an angle. "We had a deal!"

"Sorry, kid." Elmore stuck his lip out in an exaggerated, childish pout. "Had my fingers crossed the whole time. Better luck next—"

Elmore was interrupted by the pointed end of a silver, sparkly stiletto to the side of his neck. He screeched, blood spurting from the wound. The shoe remained there, driven deep like a sword into a stone. Elmore tried to go for a gun from beneath his jacket, but Lucy used her other shoe to strike him hard across the temple, sending him to the floor. He lay there bleeding onto the linoleum.

"What'd I tell you, huh?" Lucy yelled. "What did I fucking *tell you*, Cera?!"

The brute turned his back on Cera, appraising the new assailant dressed only in a sparkly bikini and oversized hoop earrings. She beckoned him toward her, as unflinching and outsized as a matador. Before he could charge, Cera threw herself onto his back, wrapping his arms around his neck and sinking her teeth into his ear.

"You little *bitch!*" He bucked like a mechanical bull. "I'm gonna fuckin' kill *both* of you!"

From inside her bikini top, Lucy produced a small canister of pepper spray. She unleashed an arc of burning liquid at the brute's face, drenching his eyes, nose and mouth. Droplets ricocheted into Cera's as well, forcing her to release her grasp.

"Jesus Christ!" She rubbed her eyes, which only made it worse. "Watch your aim!"

Lucy ignored her, continuing to hold down the trigger inches from the brute's face. He crashed down to his knees, clawing at his face. "Stop! Stop! Goddammit, stop!"

Cera fumbled for the nearest object and grabbed a glass lamp from Lucy's end table.

"Wait!" Lucy said. "Cera, don't—"

Cera didn't wait. Barely able to open her eyes, she blearily identified the brute's silhouette and brought the lamp down on top of his head. The glass smashed. His screaming stopped. The brute slumped down beside his boss.

Lucy sighed. "That was my grandmother's lamp, Cera."

"Shit," she spat, still rubbing her burning eyes. "I can pay for—"

"It's not about the fucking money!"

The foreign concept gave Cera pause.

"I *told you* that you needed to be more careful," Lucy continued, shaking her finger like a disapproving mother. "Now look at this mess! You're lucky Shady J is such a two-pump chump and I got back here as soon as I did."

"What about you, huh?" Cera snapped. "You dropped out of school to hook up with strangers with names like 'Shady J' for a living, and now you're gonna act like Little Miss Responsible?"

"Oh *no*! This is not about me!" Lucy fumed. "*I* use protection. *I* get tested regularly. *I* have a boss who always knows exactly where I'm gonna be. *I* carry pepper spray if anything ever goes wrong. *I'm* prepared for how I earn my living. Are you?"

"I'm an *economics student,* Lucy."

She snorted. "Like that's gonna last."

"What's that supposed to mean?"

"You ain't cut out for that square-world shit, and you know it. When's the last time you went to that internship you're supposed to be doing?"

Cera didn't respond. It had been a couple days.

"You wanna live outta other people's pockets, but you don't *get it*," Lucy continued. "Right now, you're a bit player in a place that chews up fortunes like bubblegum. Don't you understand? Millions of dollars flow through this city every *second*. The kind of people that level of wealth and power attracts..." She shuddered instinctively. "Trust me, if you understood, you wouldn't be stealing from 'em."

Cera rolled her eyes. To her ears, Lucy's lecture sounded like an adult in a Peanuts cartoon. *Wah-wah-wah-wah...*

"Fine, whatever." Lucy shook her head. "Next time you find yourself in deep shit, don't you come calling me. I tried to warn you."

"Uh-huh," Cera nodded, barely listening. "Look, maybe we should be more worried about what we're gonna do about the gangsters on your apartment floor?"

Lucy smirked. "I never said this was *my* apartment."

"It's not?"

"Technically, this shithole is in my ex-boyfriend's name..."

"Lucky us."

"Lucky us?!" Lucy stamped the floor with her manicured feet like an angry horse. "Easy for you to say! Now I have to find a new place to live because of you. In this economy!"

"Calm down, calm down..." Cera knelt down beside Elmore, removed his wallet. He had a thousand bucks on him. "Look at this. Between the two of them, that's $1,500." She conveniently left out the $3,000 she'd stolen from Duane that afternoon. "Why don't we call it, say, 70-30, and wash our hands of this whole situation?"

"*70-fucking-30?!*" Lucy went rigid with anger. "You must be out of your *goddamn* mind. Like that's even gonna cover shit. Besides, the least you can do, literally the absolute fucking least you can do, after I *saved* your ass, is a straight 50-50."

It wasn't that Cera didn't appreciate getting her ass saved. But, thing was, that was Lucy's first offer. Plus Cera was still pissed about the pepper spray. She counted quickly and split the money between both hands.

"Look, you're right. You take sixty percent..." Cera gestured with the cash in her left. "And *I'll* take forty." She gestured with the cash in her right. "Take the bigger cut. You're right, you deserve it."

She stuck out the wad of bills in her left hand. Lucy took it and stuck the billfold into her top. Cera smiled, pocketing the right.

She had switched the cuts.

After all, a woman has to have her principles.

MY HEROES HAVE ALWAYS BEEN COWBOYS

Ray had a lot of practice looking like an ass, but this latest gig was enough to test even his generous tolerance for foolishness. Decked out in cheap cow-print chaps, a fringed faux-leather vest, jangly spurs, a model six-shooter on his hip, and a ten-gallon hat tall enough to qualify as a twenty gallon, the job he'd picked up at the Lazee Cowboy Ranch and Resort had him dressed like a damn cartoon character.

"Howdy, pardners!" Ray called to the wave of new arrivals. He swallowed his embarrassment and whipped around his guitar, a cheap six-string the ranch had provided him. He took a deep breath and sang in an obnoxiously exaggerated accent:

> *"There's a place I know*
> *where the folks is kind;*
> *A ranch I know*
> *on a hot gold mine;*
> *Kick your boots right off,*
> *have a grand ole time—*
> *That's right, at the*
> *Lazeeeeeeeee Cowbooooooy!"*

There was a whistling refrain and, somehow, an astonishing *eleven* more verses. Ray wanted to kill himself, but what else was new?

He'd only taken the job to earn some traveling cash while wintering down somewhere he wouldn't freeze to death. The fact that the dude ranch offered employee lodging on-site seemed convenient, but he'd quickly realized that was a detriment, not a bonus. He was trapped here, in this geedunk tourist trap, an artificial gold rush town designed to separate yuppies from their ill-gotten dollars. As soon as winter gave way to spring, he was out of here — out of Arizona, and out of the whole damn southwest for that matter. He'd head back east, see where the road took him from there.

A city boy in designer shades, paired with leather chaps and a bolo tie, looking almost as cartoonish as Ray, stopped rolling his luggage and pulled finger guns from imaginary holsters.

"Dance, varmint, dance!" City Boy cackled, shooting at Ray's feet.

Ray obliged him, wearing a pained smile. City Boy continued onward, off toward the luxury guest suites, chuckling to himself. "Hot damn, I love this place!"

That makes one of us, buddy.

More tourists poured in. Two young boys, maybe five and six years old, ran at him with toy popguns. *Pop! Pop! Pop!*

"Wow, a real cowboy!" said one.

"He's not a cowboy," replied the other. "He's an outlaw!"

They debated this back and forth before turning back to Ray.

"Are you a cowboy or an outlaw, mister?"

They looked up at him with big, eager eyes.

Ray was only supposed to play period-appropriate songs approved by the ranch owner, Mr. Reuben Cartwright. He gave a look around to make sure the boss wasn't nearby, then started singing an old favorite — *"My Heroes Have Always Been Cowboys"* by Willie Nelson.

The two boys erupted into cheers. Ray's smile was genuine this time. A haggard woman who looked like she hadn't gotten a good night's sleep in five or six years ran up, pulling a pair of cheap suitcases.

"Boys! What did I tell you about running off on your own?"

"Mom! Mom!" they both cheered. "A real cowboy! A real cowboy!"

"Careful," Ray said. "Y'all better listen to your mama. That's what good cowboys do."

"Yes, sir!" They began running circles around their mom, firing off their guns. *Pop! Pop! Pop!*

Thank you, mouthed the tired-eyed woman. Ray tipped his hat to her.

"Come on, boys, let's leave the nice man alone…"

They headed off toward the value rooms, on the other half of the ranch away from the luxury suites. He was still watching her walk away when a voice sounded at his shoulder.

"Decided you're too good to sing to greet our guests?"

Ray jumped and spun back around.

"N-no, Mr. Cartwright, not at all…"

Cartwright — a well-built man with a golden pocket watch, little calculating eyes, a pin-striped suit, and a hat even taller than Ray's — gave him a smile of nicotine-yellowed teeth. He hocked a tobacco-chew loogie at Ray's feet.

"That's what I thought, boy. Hop to."

Ray took a deep breath.

> *"There's a town I know*
> *built 'round a rush of gold;*
> *And a saloon I go*
> *where the beer is cold;*
> *Where the day is young*
> *and the living's old —*
> *That's right, at the*
> *Lazeeeeeeeee Cowbooooooy!"*

• • •

The whole 'gold mine' thing was bullshit, of course.

Yes, the Lazee Cowboy Ranch and Resort was built on top of an old mine, but anything valuable had been scraped out of the earth a long time ago. Instead, the shafts were lined by veins of pyrite — fool's gold that tourists paid real money to extract themselves, play-acting miners, cowboys, and prospectors. The only person the place was a gold mine for was its owner, judging by the Corvette he drove to work each day.

"Generations of my family made their fortune here," Cartwright had said when he'd hired Ray to sing old western standards. "You stick around long enough, maybe you'll make your fortune too."

The job paid peanuts. Most of the hands spent what little cash they made in the saloon after work — just like real cowboys, trapping themselves in a loop of labor, alcoholism, and deferred dreams. When Ray took the job, he'd told himself he wouldn't drink his wages away this time. Like every other time he'd made that promise to himself, it lasted about a day.

"I'm about done with this damn place," Slim told Ray one night, drinking at the bar. "I've almost saved up enough money to get out of here for good."

Dressed in all black, Slim played a horse rustler as part of a show where the tourists could pay to be "deputized" and then catch criminals in the act, bringing them into the sheriff's for the "reward" — a coupon for 10% off their next reservation. Slim brought a certain verisimilitude to his role, being an ex-con himself. As part of his position, he spent a good half his time in the stocks in the town square, leaving him with a curve to his posture.

"Bullshit," Ray said. "If you're here every night, how much can you really have saved up?"

"You think this is all I do, greenhorn? I got myself some side hustles. A proper dee-versified port-folio."

"Oh yeah? Like what?"

Slim glanced around, making sure no one was watching. He leaned in close. Ray leaned in to match, suddenly nervous at whatever secret he was about to be let in on.

"You, uh…" Slim glanced around again. "You wanna buy some weed?"

Ray burst out laughing.

• • •

Later that night, Ray wandered the ranch grounds smoking a joint, the perfect blend of intoxications. Slim's grass was pretty good, with smoke that smelled of lemon, spice, and skunk. He whistled a Willie Nelson song in time to the jangling of his spurs.

"Howdy, pardner," came a familiar voice to his right. "Can a girl bum a smoke?"

Ray jumped and spun, hiding the joint behind his back. On a bench sat the tired-eyed woman, a gray hoodie wrapped around her against the coolness of the desert night.

"I weren't smokin'," Ray lied.

"What's behind your back, then?"

"…Not a cigarette."

Technically, not a lie.

The woman smiled, bringing a twinkle to her exhausted eyes. "I *know* it's not a cigarette. So you gonna share or what?"

"So long as you ain't a narc…"

Ray plopped down and passed over the joint. She took a hit and sighed back into the bench, exhaling contentedly.

"Ray, by the way."

"Cassie," she said, passing it back.

"So where are the boys?"

"Asleep, blessedly. These are the few hours I get any peace."

"They seem like quite the pair of little rabble rousers."

Ray kept the joint moving.

"They're good boys," she chuckled. "And lord, do they *love* cowboys. Took damn near every penny I had to my name, but when I told them when we were coming here for a few days, their screams could've shattered glass."

"Oughta to be careful. A cowboy's ramblin' life ain't all it's cracked up to be."

"Speaking from experience?"

"Yeah, and plenty of it. Only way I've ever learned any lesson in life has been the hard way."

"'*Mammas, don't let your babies grow up to be cowboys,*'" Cassie sang in a clear, crystalline voice. Ray harmonized along. They carried through an entire chorus and verse.

"Maybe you're right, but I figure I'll worry about all that a little further down the road," she said. "For now, I just wanted to give 'em something to smile about. Ever since their dad…" Cassie took a long, sad drag on the joint. "Well, nevermind that."

Ray decided to let that particular sleeping dog lie.

"A voice like that," he said, "you shoulda been a country singer."

"Ah, I never woulda made it. You though, you should be off in Nashville, not singing on some dude ranch."

He shrugged. "Sore subject. Actually tried once. It didn't go so well."

"Ain't that just life? Seems like nothing ever works out the way folks like us want."

"I guess neither of us should be here tonight, huh?" Ray looked up at the expanse of stars above the desert and the wisps of clouds, propelled by gentle winds, going only where the currents took them. "We should be off touring the country, cutting gold records, sounds like."

"Yeah, but…" Cassie put a hand on Ray's. "Here we are."

Ray looked down from the sky. Despite their exhaustion, her eyes shone brighter than the stars.

"Yeah, I guess we are…"

He leaned in slowly, giving her time to back out. She leaned in as well, meeting his lips. He pulled her in close, their kiss intensifying, but she suddenly broke off.

"I'm sorry," she whispered, looking away.

"No, fuck, I'm sorry, I shouldn't have—"

Cassie rose and fled into the night, vanishing in the darkness of desert shadow.

You really mess up everything you touch, don't you, Ray?

Ray sighed and re-lit the joint, watching the clouds in transit to their predetermined destinations and the stars beyond them, a silent audience eternally devoid of applause.

● ● ●

News of the car thefts broke the next morning.

Ray found out about it while he was in Mr. Cartwright's office in the so-called courthouse, a room decorated with assorted antiques, old glass vases filled with dead flowers, posters of famous outlaws, and framed newspaper clippings. "*New resort seeks to reinvigorate local mine's history,*" read one.

Ray was on an important mission, trying to convince Cartwright to allow him to add some more modern songs to the approved repertoire.

"It's all about making folks happy, right?" Ray argued. "So let's give 'em a few tunes they recognize — some Willie and Waylon, at least."

"Were Willie and Waylon around for the Gold Rush?"

"Well, no… but were intercoms around during the Gold Rush?" Ray pointed to the gooseneck microphone on Cartwright's desk, which connected to the speaker system Cartwright used to make announcements about the day's events. "How about that, huh?"

"You best stop questioning how I run my ranch, boy," Mr. Cartwright smoldered from beneath the brim of his tall white hat. "Or else."

Or else I won't have to wear this ridiculous get-up no more? Whatever will I do?

But before Ray could fire off a rebuttal, City Boy with the designer shades burst through the office door, hollering up a storm.

"They stole my fucking Beamer, on *your* watch!"

"Hold on, hold on, hold on," Cartwright said, "whatchu talkin' about?"

City Boy hollered on and on about how expensive his luxury BMW was, how it had been stolen right out of the lot, and how that was the ranch's responsibility.

Mr. Cartwright disagreed.

"It's a damn shame, this world we're living in," Cartwright shook his head, tsking his tongue sadly. "But you may recall from the paperwork you signed…" He pointed to a sign above the door.

LAZEE COWBOY RANCH IS NOT LIABLE FOR ANY LOST OR STOLEN PROPERTY.

"So, unless you need to pay for a few more days while you figure out how to get out of here, I'm not sure how much help I can be here."

City Boy grumbled beneath his breath, handing over a credit card.

"Highway fucking robbery…"

Ray couldn't give two shits about City Boy's bank account or his precious BMW. He was about to relaunch into his Willie and Waylon argument when a second figure burst through Mr. Cartwright's door. Rather than the beet-red anger of his previous visitor, this newcomer took a different approach — tears and desperation.

"They stole the battery and catalytic converter right out of my car," Cassie wailed, pointedly avoiding eye contact with Ray. "Who would do such an awful thing?"

"Auto rustlers," Mr. Cartwright shrugged. "If the whole car's not worth taking, they just strip some of the easy-to-grab pieces."

"But what am I supposed to *do*?"

"I don't rightly know, but unless you pay for any extra days you spend here, I'm gonna have to have you escorted off the property. And we wouldn't want that now, would we?"

Tears rolled freely down her cheeks. "I can't *afford* that," she sobbed. "I emptied my damn bank account just to bring my boys here in the first fucking place."

Cartwright shrugged. "All due respect, ma'am, but that ain't my problem."

"I'll pay it," Ray interjected.

"What's that, boy?"

"However long she's here until she figures stuff out, just take it outta my paychecks."

Cartwright chuckled. "I don't think you appreciate how much this fine, all-inclusive establishment *costs* to stay here. Even a couple days in the value suites. You'll be working off the debt for months."

"Fine. Whatever. Then I'll work it off for months."

The boss man shrugged. "Suit yourself. They're your wages."

Cassie rose and left the room in a huff. Ray followed her outside.

"Hold on, Cassie, wait up…"

She rounded on him. "I didn't need anything from you!"

"Wait, wha?"

"I'm not some fucking damsel in distress for you to save," Cassie snapped. "Everything I have, I've fought tooth and nail for, my-god-damn-self. I don't need nobody's pity!"

"Ain't a drop of pity here," Ray promised. "Just tryin' to lend a helpin' hand, that's all…"

"Well, keep your hands to your goddamn self." Cassie spat at his boots. "Me and my boys got no need for you, *or* your help."

Ray watched her storm away, back toward her room on the cheap half of the ranch.

"Jesus Christ," he muttered, "I need a drink…"

• • •

"Oh, it happens from time to time. Sometimes a couple times a season." Louie, the mustachioed barkeep, cleaned a glass as he spoke, barely paying Ray's questions any mind. "Rumor has it, it's some sort of auto ring out of Phoenix."

Ray guzzled a pint of beer, burping loud enough to rattle the windows. "That's more'n an hour away. Why would they come all the way out here?"

Louie shrugged. "Just somethin' I heard Mr. Cartwright say."

"And the police never turn nothin' up?"

"Hell, police around here are worth about as much as a second asshole in your armpit."

"That sure sounds like the cops, alright…"

"There's no cameras in the parking lot. So they usually just shrug, say the ranch oughta install some, then get back to wasting taxpayer dollars."

"And after all this, there still ain't no cameras?"

Louie shrugged. "Cartwright's a money-grubbing old bastard." His face reddened. "Don't tell him I said that, o' course…"

Slim cut in, nursing a morning pint of his own. "I thought you ain't had a car. What you so worried about?"

"Oh, nothin," Ray shrugged. "Just a curious person by nature, I suppose."

"Oughta be careful. Ain't you heard about curiosity and the cat?"

Ray squinted at Slim.

After his liquid breakfast, Ray listened in on the ranch gossip, dropping eaves on tourists from around corners and behind barrels. Half a dozen cars had been hit, they said. Nicer vehicles had been stolen outright, hijacked and driven right off the lot. Some of the cheaper cars, like Cassie's, had a few parts nicked, a simple way for the thieves to inflate their score.

Ray took a walk around the lot to inspect things for himself. Mr. Cartwright's gleaming, sunset-orange Corvette still sat in its prized parking space, untouched by the thieves. Ray found that an interesting oversight.

What are you fixin' to do now, you dumbass?

His answer: *Sumpthin' fucking stupid, per usual…*

That night, Ray removed his spurs and snuck out of the employee quarters to watch the parking lot, peering out from behind a large rock with a convenient line of sight. No one came. He passed out at some point, leaning up against the stone. He went to work again the next morning, back aching. More tourists arrived, seeking the gold and glory of an imagined west. The shows and storylines continued on as usual. He caught sight of Cassie and her boys once but she avoided eye contact, hurrying her kids along.

The next evening, Ray returned to his stakeout spot. The desert night deepened. He'd nearly slipped into sleep once more when a noise roused him. He peered out and saw a shadowed figure stalking from car to car. Even in the darkness, he could make out the silhouette of the thief's rounded posture.

Hiya Slim, ya fuckin' rustler.

It occurred to Ray he hadn't thought out his next move. His plans usually fell apart before yielding any fruit, so why bother thinking them through? He'd do what he always did — improvise, like throwing together a blues solo between a couple verses.

He snuck down through the lot, glad he'd had the foresight to remove his spurs. Slim was hard at work jimmying a metal appendage in the door of a luxury SUV when Ray pressed the barrel of his model gun against the back of his skull.

"Listen here, outlaw," Ray growled, adopting an exaggerated voice to conceal his identity. "Drop it, step back from the car, and don't turn around."

Slim paused, but didn't drop his jimmying tool. Ray cocked the fake hammer from dramatic effect.

"I *said*, reach for the sky, and step away from the car."

Slim titled his head. "That you, Ray?"

Ray cleared his throat. "...*No?*"

"Curiosity got the better of you, eh, greenhorn? Boss ain't gonna like this." He tsked his tongue. "I tried to warn you."

Ray returned to his real voice. "You said you were almost out of here, Slim. What happens if you get caught, huh?"

"Don't you fucking lecture me," Slim snapped. "This is *how* I get out. You don't know what it's like, being trapped in this shithole for *years*."

"You realize I ain't just gonna let this go, right?"

Ray still had the fake gun pressed against his head. Slim turned enough to glance back over his shoulder.

"And *you* know I realize that ain't a real gun, right?"

"Oh shi—"

Ten paces. Draw! Fire!

Slim spun around, swinging the metal at Ray's face. Ray took an instinctive step backwards, the jimmy coming within inches of his eyes, then moved forward again, swinging wildly with the gun. The metal cracked across Slim's temple, sending him down to the ground, unconscious.

Ray spun his six-shooter by the trigger guard and blew imaginary smoke from the barrel.

"Fastest gun in the west."

He patted Slim down, finding a set of lock picks in a vest pocket. Ray confiscated them before dragging Slim to the nurse's station. He pounded the door, then bolted. He watched from around the corner to make sure he got taken inside.

Something Slim said kept bouncing around Ray's brain. *'Boss ain't gonna like this.'* He turned it over and over and kept coming to the same conclusion.

There was only one boss at the Lazee Cowboy Ranch and Resort. *Strike while the iron's hot, right?*

Ray tip-toed through the night toward Cartwright's office, avoiding the tourists still up playing midnight cowboy. He passed City Boy, drunk outside the saloon, ranting to somebody on his phone.

"I swear, I'd sue the chaps right off of 'em if I could… Hot damn, I hate it here…"

Now we're on the same page.

Ray resisted the temptation to interrupt him with a pair of finger guns, shouting *"dance, varmint, dance!"* He considered it an admirable exercise in restraint.

He also snuck past Cassie, sitting out on the same bench from the other night. She too was on the phone.

"I'm sorry, I didn't know who else to call… I figure even *you* wouldn't want us stranded out here like this…"

Ray, once again, decided to let that particular sleeping dog lie.

When he reached the imitation courthouse, Ray lingered in the shadows until the coast was clear of prying eyes. He took Slim's lockpicks from his pocket and got to work. Turned out, lockpicks were not a magic ticket for opening doors. More than once, approaching footsteps forced him to hide, the picks still sticking out from the lock. Thankfully, the tourists remained oblivious. Finally, after much cursing, he forced the mechanism to unlock.

Holding his breath, he pushed the door open. No alarm sounded.

So far, so good…

He closed the door behind him and flipped the light switch.

Problem was, Ray wasn't sure what he was looking for. He flipped through the assorted papers on Cartwright's desk scattered around the microphone: invoices, employee contracts, guest registrations… Nothing that seemed out of the ordinary.

He dug through the desk drawers, yielding nothing of interest. The bottom drawer, however, was locked. Ray jimmied the metal picks in the keyhole. This time, with no tourists to interrupt his clandestine efforts, he made faster work of the mechanism. The drawer popped open.

It was empty.

What the fuck?

That didn't make any sense. Who else would Slim be working for if not for Cartwright? Why have a locked drawer with nothing in it? More out of stubbornness than anything else, Ray felt around the drawer by hand, refusing to believe he'd hit a dead end. At the very back, barely noticeable, he felt a small lip to the wood. By his nails, he clawed the false bottom out of place.

This time, Ray struck gold.

There were two ledgers inside the drawer. Ray wasn't a numbers guy, but he could tell that in one set of books, the ranch was bleeding money — barely staying afloat during the busy season, and on the verge of perpetual collapse during the slower months. Yet in the other set of books, the ranch was a resounding success. Some ups and downs, sure, but a far sight from the impending financial ruin reflected in its doppelganger.

There it is. Cartwright's cooking the books, keeping this place alive on dirty money.

But why? The very thing that Cartwright was using to breathe life into his precious ranch could easily, with one wrong move, be the very thing that undid it. So why take the risk?

Unfortunately for Ray, his musings were cut short.

The doorknob turned. Ray barely had enough time to shove the books back into the drawer before the door opened. Cartwright entered, wearing an ugly smile like an outlaw's bandanna.

"Why, M-M-Mr. Cartwright," Ray stammered, glancing around the room, trying to formulate a plan. "What are you doing here so late?"

"Now, now, boy," the ranch owner drawled. "That's *my* line. Just what in the hell do you think you're doin'?"

"I was, uh… looking for where you keep the approved song list." His eyes briefly registered a detail on Cartwright's desk, but he snapped his gaze back up to the ranch owner. "I was, uh, just gonna add some Wille Nelson, yeah…"

"That so?"

Cartwright lumbered around the office circling toward Ray, still standing at the desk. Each footfall shook the room, Cartwright's spurs ringing like little tambourines. Ray remained exactly where he was.

"That's some lengths to go through for a country song."

"What can I say? Shotgun Willie, man. He's the fuckin' best."

Cartwright stepped up to Ray, close enough to bump Ray's chest with his girth. Ray still remained unmoved. Cartwright's little eyes glanced down to his bottom desk drawer. It stood slightly ajar. The ranch owner's eyes traveled back up to Ray, the false warmth he adopted for the tourists replaced by something distant and cold.

"I got an interesting call from the nurse tonight," Cartwright said.

Ray played dumb. He was good at that.

"Oh?"

"Said Slim had been dropped off at the door with a brand-spanking-new concussion. Then I see the lights on in my office. You wouldn't know anything about Slim, would you now?"

"Not an inkling, sir."

Cartwright chuckled. "Your poker face ain't the worst I've ever seen, but you're in too deep now. So why don't we dispense with this little game?"

"I can't rightly say I follow, sir."

"You're clearly much more of an enterprising individual than I initially took you for. A man with your drive, why, we could do good business together. You see what I'm saying?"

Play it careful…

"Even if I was pickin' up what you're puttin' down — and I ain't sayin' I am — I gotta know. Why go through all this trouble for this little ole place?" *Now lay it on thick.* "A man with your brains, you could make twice as much somewhere else, easy."

Cartwright pursed his lips, considering Ray's question. He mosied away from Ray toward the window behind his desk, through which moonlight streamed.

As soon as Cartwright's back was turned, Ray flipped the switch that activated the microphone on his desk. The little red light beside the mic blinked on. Ray carefully covered it with one of the invoices scattered across the desk. Cartwright gazed through glass up at the desert stars and the wisps of clouds on their way to whatever predestinations awaited them.

"Do you have *family*, Raymond?"

It was the first time Ray could remember that Cartwright had actually used his name since hiring him.

"Not in any meaningful sense, no…"

"Then you don't understand what it means to be a part of a *legacy*. The burden of a man's *bloodline*."

Ray didn't interrupt. Cartwright was building to something.

"My pappy worked this mine. His pappy before him worked the

mine. And *his* pappy before *him* worked the mine. A legacy, inherited from generation to generation. And what do I inherit?"

Cartwright turned back around, his lip curled into a snarl. Ray casually leaned back against the desk, blocking his view of the microphone.

"A hollow vein, already bled dry. All my family's legacy, reduced to dust and fool's gold. So what's a man to do?"

"Whatever a man's got to."

"See? I knew you'd understand. Exactly. A man does what he's got to do for his bloodline. So that's exactly what I done. I built a new empire, one that breathes life into the past to help folks escape the present. I'm giving these people somethin' they *need*."

"But folks ain't so interested in the past anymore, are they? There's a brave new world out there, all shiny and chrome."

"These people, they don't understand what we've lost. They think having a car stolen is some great loss? Their history, the very legacy of our forefathers, is slipping between our fingers like dirt through a prospector's pan."

Ray didn't bother mentioning the little detail about how that same idealized history was built on slavery, on violence, on barbarity, on injustice and indignity. It would only throw Cartwright off his groove. He was so close. *Just push a little farther...*

"So you do what you gotta do."

Cartwright again stepped close enough to push against Ray with his girth. Again, Ray remained in place, his casual demeanor belying his heart thundering up into his throat.

"You're goddamn right. I do exactly what I need to keep this place alive, because they *need it*. Because if I let this place die, I let our past die with it. Ain't never had a woman who would take me, ain't got no children. *This place* is my bloodline. And I'd gladly steal a thousand more cars from these clueless fuckin' city slickers if it means this mine lives on."

Jackpot. Talk about fool's gold.

Ray just let him keep digging his hole.

"So that leaves you with two options," Cartwright said. "Either you come with me while the gettin's good and make yourself some easy money. Or…" His face darkened like a sky filled by storm clouds. "You make yourself into a problem, and I bury you so deep in that goddamn mine you'll be a lump of fucking coal before someone digs you back up."

Ray gulped.

Cartwright pressed even closer. "So what'll it be? Choice is yours, boy."

"I never done good with ultimatums," Ray shrugged. "How about a third option?"

"There ain't no third option. And I ain't presenting the choices again. If you don't pick, I will. And you won't like the one I choose."

"Oh, that's okay, I don't think you're gonna like my idea either…"

Ray swept the paper off of the little light next to the microphone switch. The color bled from Cartwright's face like mine drainage seeping into previously unspoiled countryside.

"You— you—"

Ray gave him his best shit-eating grin. "Told you, you wouldn't like it."

A vein pulsed in Cartwright's temple. The color suddenly came rushing back: purplish-red, hot, violent, unthinking rage.

Uh-oh. Maybe I didn't think this through all the way…

Ray tried to run, but Cartwright was too close. He had his fat hands clasped around Ray's throat before he could get away.

"You… goddamn… yellow-bellied… little… *bastard!*"

Cartwright sprayed spittle on Ray's face, squeezing tighter and tighter. He scratched at Cartwright's face, to no avail. Darkness ate at the edges of his vision.

So this is it, huh?

This was where the winds had pushed his cloud. He shouldn't've been surprised. Nothing in life ever worked out the way he hoped. All his life, all his travels, every road he'd hitchhiked down, had brought him here.

Every road's gotta end somewhere.

He closed his eyes.

• • •

When he opened his eyes again, Ray was in a white room, wearing white robes. A red headed stranger he almost recognized was rolling a joint.

"Is this Heaven?"

"I don't think so," the stranger said. "They ain't rolled me up yet."

The stranger passed the joint over. Ray lit up, savoring the most delicious weed he'd ever tasted.

"So am I dead?"

"That's not for me to say. Above my pay grade."

"I'm pretty sure this what bein' dead feels like." Ray handed the joint back. "Were my choices worth it, if they brought me here?"

"What do you think?"

"I think I'd rather die with my middle finger in some bastard's face than live taking dirty money from a crooked fuck."

"Then you only did what you had to do."

"And now I ain't growin' old."

The sound of glass crashing, muffled and distant, echoed through the white room. The stranger gave a mischievous chuckle.

"I wouldn't be so sure of that."

"What?"

"It's time for you to go."

"I don't understand. Go where?"

"On the road again." The stranger waved. "Now you've been on both sides of goodbye."

• • •

Glass crashed.

Pressure released.

Ray gasped for air, catapulting back to consciousness. He was… alive? Still in Cartwright's office, sprawled out on his desk.

What the hell is happening?

"You little bitch!" Cartwright roared.

Ray turned toward the sound. Blood ran in rivulets down Cartwright's face, bits of glass glinting from little gashes. Cassie stood before him, holding a second antique vase.

Cartwright lunged for her, but she was too quick for him. She ducked under his arms, letting Cartwright's momentum carry him past her, then brought the vase down against the back of his head. He slumped forward onto the desk beside Ray.

Cassie brought her hands to Ray's face. "Are you okay?!"

"Look at that…" Ray chuckled weakly. "Guess *I* was the damsel who needed saving…"

Cassie shook her head, but a smile tugged at her lips. "You know you're a fucking idiot, right?"

"I might've heard that a time or two, yeah…"

The rest of the night was a blur. Police arrived at some point. Dozens of tourists recounted Cartwright's admissions over the speaker to the cops, including a particularly enthusiastic City Boy. Cartwright roused back to the awareness while the paramedics were cleaning his wounds, a pair of cuffs fastened around his wrists. Words like grand theft auto, racketeering, tax fraud, assault, and attempted murder were all thrown around.

"You have the right to remain silent…" They shoved Cartwright into the back of a cruiser, fitting in Slim beside him. "You have the right to an attorney…"

"Hey Cartwright!" Ray called, still wearing his cow-print chaps and unable to resist a final jab. "Your cowboy uniforms look fuckin' *stupid*, by the way!"

Cartwright shot Ray a glare that could've curdled milk.

"Do you, um…" Cassie glowed an embarrassed pink. "Want some company tonight?"

For the first time in a long time, Ray slept in someone else's arms.

Nothing physical transpired. That was okay. Instead, he wept into her chest.

"It's okay," she repeated, over and over. "It's okay…"

He couldn't remember the last time someone had told him that.

* * *

He awoke to the sound of Cassie's boys hollering. The bed beside him was empty. He pulled himself upright, his head throbbing bloody murder.

Almost dying will do that to you, I guess.

In the next room, Ray found that Cassie had her family's bags all packed. "I really am sorry," she was saying, "dragging you out here like this…" The boys were head over heels to see a newcomer, a man with features just like theirs. Ray put two and two together. Cassie turned, saw Ray, and glowed embarrassed pink all over again.

"Oh, Ray, this is…"

"Yeah, think I figured it out."

The father regarded Ray with suspicion and disgust. "Who the fuck's this asshole?"

"Nobody, really," Ray answered for himself. "Just some wannabe cowboy." He turned to Cassie. "Thanks for everything. Especially the 'saving-my-life' part."

"You don't have to—"

"I really do, actually." He knelt to address the boys one last time. "Hey, you two. Remember what I said. Good cowboys listen to their mammas." He glanced up at their dad. "And their papas."

"Yes, sir!" They fired off their toy guns. *Pop! Pop! Pop!*

"I think it'd be best if you got the hell out of here," their father advised.

"We might have more in common than you think," Ray said, "'cause I was just thinking the same thing."

He pushed past them into the harsh, unforgiving light of morning. The dirt crunching underfoot, he began hiking toward the employee lodgings to gather his few worldly possessions. Footsteps sounded behind him.

"Wait," Cassie called. "No goodbye? Nothing?"

Ray could hardly bear to face her. "Never been good at goodbyes, no matter what side of 'em I was on."

"Where are you even going?"

He shrugged. "Anywhere but here seems like a good start."

"What about how a cowboy's ramblin' life ain't all it's cracked up to be?"

"I can't help it," Ray said. "My heroes have always been cowboys."

"I know the song."

He smiled. "I know you do."

Unable to bring himself to say goodbye, she watched him walk away. It was the only thing he knew how to do, the only life he knew how to live, even if it never worked out the way he wanted. He pressed forever onward, driving forward like a cowboy across the plains of his misspent life, tumbling wherever the winds blew him next.

PASSING

Lilly's father threw the bag of needles at her feet. Behind him, her mother wept quietly into her hands.

"You wanna tell us what this is all about?"

Anything would've been better than the truth.

Anything.

"D-Drugs," Lilly stammered.

"Drugs?" her father spat. His lips curled into a sneer beneath his unkempt mustache.

"I-I I fell in with a bad crowd… a while back, at a party, somebody had some, and I—"

Her father interrupted with a backhand across her face, hard enough to send Lilly stumbling sideways.

"Don't you fucking lie to me, boy!"

"I'm not—"

From a pocket, her father pulled a small glass vial. *Estradiol*, read the label. They'd found that too. Nausea roiled within her stomach.

"Don't think we're fucking stupid."

Lilly's mother wailed like a police siren. "How *could* you, Billy? How could you do this?"

"We know what it is," her father growled. "What you've been doing to yourself."

Lilly stammered, her face still burning. "I-I-I…"

Her mother continued screeching. "What did we *ever do* to you, Billy? What did we do to deserve *this?*"

Because, of course, this was all about *them*.

"I can't believe it." Her father shook his head, and when he spoke again, it was in a voice curdled by disgust. " My own fucking son."

He flung the vial at the wall. The glass shattered. Something inside her shattered with it. The hormones that should've been her birth-right crawled uselessly down the wallpaper.

"You're *sick!*" her mother shrieked. "But we'll help you! We'll help you get better!"

"I'm *not* sick!" Lilly tried to explain. She really did. "This is who I *am*. Who I've *always* been. All I want is to be your daught—"

Her father struck her in the face again, this time with a closed fist. Everything went white. When her vision came back into focus, the room had turned on its side. She sat up slowly, gingerly fingering the bruise already swelling her eye shut.

"Who did this to you?" Her father roared, beet red, veins popping, spittle spraying. "Did one of those pedophile teachers groom you? I swear to god, I will *kill them*, and I will *kill you*. Do you understand?"

Her mother wrapped herself around her father's forearm. "No! Don't hurt him! Don't hurt my baby boy!"

Lilly tried to stand, but stumbled back down to her knees. On instinct, she crawled away, trying to escape her father's violence. The hulking figure followed, barely slowed by her screaming mother hanging from his arm.

"Please," Lilly begged, desperate. She didn't know what else she could say. "Please…"

"No son of mine is going to be some fucking faggot! Some fuck-ing tranny!"

"Don't hurt him! We can fix him! We can fix him!"

She kept crawling, kept begging.

"Please…"

Even if she could choke out anything coherent, what else could she say? How could she undo decades of deliberate disinformation? The malicious mythmaking of fictitious predators in women's restrooms and athletics perpetuated by soft-palmed politicians and millionaire pundits? The casual dehumanization pushed by writers and comedians from behind the comfort of their privilege for cheap laughs and cheaper thrills? The vitriol disguised as virtue festering out from behind tens of thousands of pulpits across the nation, week by week by week?

She couldn't.

It was too much.

It was all she could manage to shield her head from the blows and beg.

"Please… please… please…"

• • •

Next thing Lilly knew, she was sitting on a curb outside the McDonald's downtown, where the Nansemond riverfront passed by Main Street. Golden hour sun streaked the Virginia sky in bronze and copper above Suffolk's mixture of faded colonial architecture and gaudy new construction. Her backpack sat on the curb beside her. Lilly blinked and shook her aching head, wondering how much time she'd lost.

She concentrated. Hazy images unwillingly resurfaced.

Her father telling her she was no longer welcome, that if she ever came back, he would gut her like an animal. Her mother begging to send her to a conversion camp instead. Her father screaming he was putting an end to it, then and there, and storming off to the garage where he kept his shotgun.

Miraculously, her go-bag stuffed with razors, makeup and femme clothing had remained undiscovered, taped to the underside of her bed. She grabbed it and she ran. Buckshot echoed behind her as she sprinted away.

Lilly dragged herself into the McDonald's to compose herself in the restroom. She looked between both options, equally nauseous at the thought of getting clocked in the women's or degrading herself by using the men's. She chose the women's, and locked the door behind her.

In the mirror, she found her eye swollen completely shut, the flesh around it pulpy and purple like a rotten plum. Her chestnut hair, grown out to shoulder length, framed her face in what she thought of as a cute, feminine way. She'd always taken more after her mother's slender frame than her father's broad, stocky build, for which she was glad. Lilly knew "passing" was just more cisgender-normative nonsense — a bullshit standard many trans people didn't event *want* to indulge — but one she couldn't help but desire anyway. The hormones had begun to soften the lines of her face, but this late in the day, little pinpricks of stubble stippled her chin and cheeks. The feel of them, like sandpaper beneath her fingertips, made her want to cry again. But she didn't have time for more tears.

Lilly checked her phone. Luckily, it still worked. She didn't know how long she had until her father canceled her service. She opened up her queer shitposting group, a loose gang of folx scattered around Virginia she'd found online, and tapped out a message with trembling thumbs.

"Well, little gay people who live in my phone, it happened. My parents found out."

The chat exploded with messages of support, asking how it went.

"Currently messaging y'all from a McDonald's bathroom, newly homeless, so… not well."

Sympathies flooded her phone. "Call the Trevor Lifeline!" somebody posted. "They saved me and can do the same for you!" Another person shared their tips for homelessness. "I know it seems daunting, but people survive this all the time. You will too!" Modest sums were transferred over cash-sharing apps. "Just be glad you're not down in Texas or Florida," somebody else said. "They have it way worse down there." The chat quickly devolved into an argument, lambasting them for being so rude during a time of crisis. Lilly had no emotional bandwidth to process any of it.

A direct message came in from Rose, the closest of her online friends. They'd spent long hours gaming together, counting down the days until they started at Virginia Commonwealth University that fall, daydreaming of when they could finally be out from under their parents and be themselves full-time. Quietly, Lilly dreamed of more together, but couldn't fathom anyone ever feeling the same about her.

"Honeyyy I am so sorry!" Rose wrote.

"We were so close! Only a couple more weeks until I was going to move out anyway."

"Listen to me, everything is going to be okay."

"I should've just fucking waited to start HRT. Stupid! So stupid!"

"No, no," Rose wrote. "It's not stupid to want to be yourself. It's never stupid."

"But what am I supposed to do now?"

"Actually… I have an idea."

"What?"

"Come up to Richmond. Why wait anymore? Let's be together now."

Lilly's heart fluttered. *Be together.* Did Rose mean…?

She googled the distance.

"That's over 80 miles! How am I supposed to make it there?"

"I'll steal my dad's car after he goes to sleep. I'll meet you partway. Just start up the 460. I'll find you."

"Where will we stay until the dorms open? Not with your parents."

"I don't know, but we'll figure it out together. Ok?"

There Rose went, using that word again. So much of Lilly's youth had been defined by isolation. Did she know how to be 'together' with someone, in *any* sense of the word? Her thumbs hesitated over the screen.

"Okay," Lilly wrote. "Let's do it."

Rose sent back a dozen hearts.

Lilly flushed embarrassed pink.

"Conserve your battery," Rose said. "Keep me updated where you are."

"Thank you, Rosie."

"You're gonna make it through this. We are gonna make it through this. Everything will be okay."

In the bathroom's flickering light, her swollen and unshaven face stared back at her from the graffiti-scratched mirror, a distorted visage that drowned her in dysphoria. It felt hard to believe that anything ever *could* be okay.

"I know," Lilly replied, trying to have faith anyway. "I know it will."

She returned the phone to her pocket and brooded over her dysphoric reflection. She couldn't do anything about the black eye, but the stubble she could manage. She popped the top off her shaving cream, but a rattling came at the bathroom door. An angry voice sounded outside.

"Who's in there locking the goddamn bathroom door? There's four fucking stalls!"

Panic rising in her chest, she stowed her shaving tools. From a pocket, she pulled a pandemic mask and hid the lower half of her face. Suddenly, she saw herself, instead of the boy she was never supposed to be. She placed her fingertips to the glass, wishing she could slip through it to the other side, to a mirror world where she had always been herself. The door shook again.

"Hello!? Other people have to go!"

She unlocked the door and rushed out, her head downcast to conceal her face from the woman outside.

"Bitch," she muttered.

Despite the insult, Lilly smiled beneath her mask. Even if it was only for a brief moment, with her face obscured, it meant she'd passed.

• • •

The peanut farms stretched out beside the highway into the long, dark night of the south. Lightning bugs flickered skyward above the black expanses. Lilly imagined they were stars fallen to earth, trying to return home. Little dreams borne upward by the summer breeze beneath their wings, only to be betrayed by the cruelty of gravity — beautiful, but forever separated from their heavenly kin, trapped down on the ground with the rest of the animals. But Lilly didn't see why that should matter. They were stars to her.

An eighteen-wheeler screamed down the highway. She flattened herself against the guardrail, wincing as the truck whipped by. The gale of displaced air almost threatened to lift her and take her someplace else. She wished it would.

Tail lights vanished into the darkness. She kept walking. Lilly opened her messages to check in with Rose, but her phone no longer had any service. How would they find each other now? A river of tears once again threatened to overflow the banks of her eyelids. But lacking any alternative, she kept moving forward.

The hum of a new vehicle sounded behind her. She pressed against the guardrail, wiping her eyes with her sleeve. A maroon sedan passed by, but the brake lights glowed and the car pulled off to the shoulder, hazard lights flashing. Lilly's breath caught in her throat. Whatever a stranger might want with her, alone at night on the side of the highway, it couldn't be good. She turned around and started walking away.

A middle-aged woman in an understated pantsuit emerged from the car. "Honey?" she called. "Honey, are you alright?"

Lilly didn't answer. The woman jogged to catch up to her.

"What are you doing out alone like this?"

"I'm fine," Lilly said, not turning around. "Don't worry about me."

"It's not safe, walking alone at night like this. A young girl like yourself. It's dangerous!"

Lilly's heart fluttered. *A young girl like yourself.*

She turned to the woman, her one eye wide. The woman gasped at the sight of the bruise that had swollen the other shut.

"My God! What happened?"

Lilly instinctively covered her face with one hand. "Nothing! I said don't worry about me." Her voice wavered. "I'm *fine*, okay?"

"Honey, oh, honey," the woman cooed. "Who did this? Your boyfriend?"

"My father," Lilly scowled.

"The bastard…!" Sympathy and rage colored the woman's face in equal measure. "Little men with empty hearts, trying to fill the hole inside themselves with violence. And it's *us* who bear the brunt of their abuse."

She extended her arms to embrace Lilly. In spite of herself, Lilly took a step back. The woman let her arms fall, not pressing it.

"Please, let me help you," she pleaded.

"You don't even *know* me."

"I *was* you once. I've been where you are."

Lilly wanted to believe her. But here, all alone, with someone she didn't know — it was too dangerous.

"No," Lilly said, firmly. "I'll be okay."

"Please, dear, let me—"

"I said no!"

Sadness replaced the sympathy in her eyes. "You're strong. I see that. But you don't have to do this alone."

Lilly stared at her shoes.

"Look, if you won't let me help you… There's a shelter in the next town. The Windsor Women's Shelter. I can even take you there. They can help you, if you let them."

Lilly remained intensely interested in her Converse.

"It's okay. I get it. You've been hurt. You have every right to keep your guard up. But… please, let them help you. You deserve it, okay?"

She took a step forward and placed a hand on her shoulder.

This time, Lilly didn't fight it.

"You are a strong and beautiful young woman," the woman said. "No matter what anyone tells you."

Lilly waited until the woman's taillights had been enveloped by darkness before moving again. She wanted to fall to her knees in tears, but she didn't have time to marinate in self-pity. For all she knew, the woman might call the cops, thinking she was helping — as if the police had historically been friends to the underdogs, the underprivileged, and the underserved.

She pressed forward into the nighttime.

Beside the highway, the lightning bugs blinked upwards into the darkness.

• • •

Windsor huddled around the parallel lines where highway and train tracks mirrored each other. Used auto lots, garages, gas stations, hardware stores, and family restaurants stood crammed between the two modes of travel, both delivering passengers and freight to whatever destinations awaited them. Lilly envied the certainty of a passing train, rumbling confidently into the future. She could only hope she would arrive in Richmond, into Rose's waiting arms, with the same certainty.

The Windsor Women's Shelter stood sandwiched between two churches. Like its neighbors, its sign bore a prominent cross. "That which you have done for the least of these," it read, "you have done for me."

She froze, petrified. The highway woman's words echoed in her mind.

A strong and beautiful young woman. No matter what anyone tells you.

For the second time that night, Lilly had been acknowledged as her true self. A simple honor most take for granted, but one she'd had to fight for. The body and name she'd been given at birth didn't matter. She *was* a woman, and if there was a God, it was Him who made Her one. She *belonged* here, as much as any woman in need of shelter.

She timidly entered. A woman about her mother's age, in a

discount blouse and Wal-Mart jewelry, looked up from behind a front desk. "Clarice," a nametag advised. At the sight of Lilly's face, she gasped.

Lilly swallowed hard. Had she been clocked?

"You sweet thing," Clarice said. "What happened to you?"

She breathed a sigh of relief. "M-my father," Lilly said, careful to remember her voice training. "He kicked me out, and, well…" She gestured to her swollen eye.

"Don't you worry about a thing." Clarice shuffled out from behind the desk. "We'll get you cleaned up and fed and settled, and in the morning, we'll get you all fixed up with a case manager, talk through the needs of your situation. How's that sound?"

She took Lilly gently around the shoulder and began steering her back.

"I, um… I have a friend on the way down from Richmond to get me. I just need a bathroom, a way to message her that I'm here, and a space to wait until she gets here…"

"We'll at least need you to fill out some intake paperwork," Clarice advised.

"Paperwork?" Lilly's stomach turned at the thought of her legal name.

"Of course, dearie, so we can best assist you. For now, though, let's get you to that bathroom…"

She steered Lilly through a common room boasting a TV set to quiet static, shelves stacked with books, racks of non-profit pamphlets, and women from all walks of life sleeping on every available couch and chair. "All our beds are full," Clarice half-explained, half-apologized. "But we don't like to turn any woman away. Ah, here we are."

The restroom was communal, with three sinks and half a dozen stalls. Lilly's heart shuddered inside her ribcage.

"Is there nowhere else that's a little more… private?"

Clarice shrugged, again half-apologizing. "Sorry, dearie, not really. Lotta women come through these doors; we have to be able to accommodate. But at this hour, I think we're the only ones still up." She gave Lilly a gentle nudge onward. "You should have it to yourself."

Lilly nodded nervously, closing the bathroom door behind her. She checked each stall before she got started. Producing her shaving equipment from her go-bag, she placed her mask into a pocket and lathered her face. The water refused to get hot, forcing her to shave in slow, deliberate strokes to avoid cutting herself. She had just begun on her chin, the trickiest part of her face, when she heard the sound of someone yawning and rising out in the common room. Then footsteps, approaching the bathroom.

Shit. Shit. Shit.

Lilly threw her razor and cream back into her bag, her heartbeat pounding in her ears. A faceful of shaving cream would get her clocked without doubt.

She lifted a scoopful of water to rinse away the foam, then a second, but it was too late. The door was already creaking open.

At the threshold of the bathroom stood a girl about Lilly's age, dressed in tattered PJ pants and a hand-me-down hoodie. Their eyes met, Lilly's filled with fear; the girl's filled with sleepy confusion. The girl blinked.

Maybe she wouldn't say anything, too tired and too focused on emptying her bladder before returning to sleep. The girl blinked a second time, still looking.

Or maybe she would understand. There were good people, true allies, out in the wilds. She was young enough, right? Maybe she would be cool.

She blinked a third time. The girl adopted a new expression.

It was anger.

"No, wait," Lilly tried to preempt her. "Please—"

"Why the fuck is there *a man* in here?!" the girl screamed, loud enough to wake the entire common room.

"No, I'm not. I-I'm just trans, and my family kicked me out, so—"

"Y'all let some sick-in-the-head groomer freak in here?!"

Clarice appeared over the girl's shoulder, and once again, the sight of Lilly's face caused her to gasp. Lilly could hear the difference this time.

"One of *these* things, in our shelter." Clarice steamed inside, grabbed Lilly by the wrist, and yanked. "Come along. Out you go. Out where you belong."

"No, please! No!"

Clarice dragged her back through the common room like trash to be tossed to the curb. She didn't even have time to grab her bag. Every sleeping body had risen and watched the spectacle. The hot weight of their judgment seared like irons against her skin.

"I only do this for your own good," Clarice reassured her as they approached the door. "If we indulge your delusion, we'll only further Satan's hold on you. This is an act of love, son."

"Your love is *violence*," Lilly spat back. "Just like my father's."

"Such disgusting arrogance." Clarice bristled at the comparison. "Don't worry, child. I'll pray for you to be healed of your sickness."

And with that, she ejected Lilly from the shelter like a leper from a village.

"That which you've done for the least of these, huh?!" Lilly screamed. "You fucking hypocrites!"

No reply came from beyond the door. A prayer, unanswered. Self-preservation pushed its way through her anger. The last thing she needed was them calling the cops. Lilly turned back to the main street, hoping against hope that Rose might still find her somewhere along the highway.

It'll be okay.

Please, let it be okay.

Please...

If her pleading was supposed to be a prayer, she didn't know to whom. Either God wasn't listening, couldn't help, or didn't care. So why call him God? Or maybe there was nothing out there, no one listening, only a silence greater and more eternal than any deity. She replaced her mask and pressed onward with a breaking heart, aching soul, and blistering feet. The night deepened around her.

At the edge of town, a cop car sat in a lot beside the highway, all its lights dark — an ambush predator in wait.

Lilly froze like a deer, considering bolting. But this was the only way out of town. Her only hope at finding Rose. Maybe there was nobody inside. The car *was* completely dark. And even if there was, they were probably looking for speeders. Saps they could ticket to make some easy money.

She crossed to the other side of the road and held her breath as she entered the vehicle's field of view. The car remained silent and still. She passed by with no response. Twenty feet down the road, she finally let her breath out.

Then the headlights burned to life, casting her shadow in front of her like a distorted reflection.

She walked faster. So did her shadow.

Gravel crunched beneath tires as the cop car pulled onto the highway.

She broke into a jog. Her shadow followed.

The hum of tires approached from behind. Her shadow lengthened to unnerving proportions as the lights closed in. She erupted into a sprint.

The cop car pulled up alongside her, keeping pace with ease. A window rolled down. From within, a square-jawed man with a thick rectangular mustache smiled out at her.

"What's the trouble, sunshine?"

Lilly kept running, didn't answer.

"I said, what's the trouble? I see a pretty young girl like you, running alone at night, I think to myself, that's not right. All sorts of dangers out here for a little thing like you…"

Lilly turned to look at him. She could see his eyes register the visible signs of abuse across her face, but his expression wasn't pity or sympathy. It was a smug smile, the amusement of a cat finding a mouse.

He cut her off with the car and threw it in park.

"Hey there, little girl." He stepped out, towering over her. "You keep running like that, maybe I think *you* done somethin' wrong. You don't want me to take you in, do you?"

"Please." Lilly's voice shook. "I'm just passing through. That's it."

"Just passing through?" the officer said, stepping forward.

"That's it," Lilly repeated.

The cop leaned in close enough she could smell his tobacco chew breath.

"How'd you get that bruise?"

"My father gave it to me. Why I left. I'm on my way to a friend's house. I ain't done nothing wrong."

"On your way to…?" The cop laughed, gesturing down the highway. "There ain't nothin' out there. Nothin' but night and shadow. You're a long ways from wherever's you tryin' to go."

Lilly felt like she was going to be sick. "I ain't done nothing wrong," she repeated.

He hovered his head directly beside Lilly's face. She recoiled at his hot, rotten breath assaulting her neck.

"What if I don't believe you?" He brought his mustache close enough to tickle her ear. "What then?"

Run.

Lilly tore off back the way she came, but the cop grabbed her before she could take two steps.

"Oh, you want to play it the hard way." He laughed — a cold, cruel noise. "That's okay. I like the hard way."

"No! Let me go! Let me go! You fucking animal!"

He backhanded her across the face, purposefully striking her injury. The pain made everything go white for a second. He tossed her into the backseat like a piece of cheap luggage. She dove for the door handle. There was none. The car shook as he settled himself back into the driver's seat. He pulled back onto the roadway, chuckling.

"Where are you taking me?" Lilly demanded. "The station?"

"The station? Oh, no, no, no…" He shook his head, smiling all the while. "A pretty little thing like you, I'm takin' you someplace we can come to… well, call it an *understanding*." He flashed a lecherous grin.

Lilly's brain went numb with panic. *Oh god. Oh no. Oh no.*

She thrashed in the backseat, pounding at the windows.

Please… please… please!

The cop just kept on chuckling, pulling off onto some dirt access road. "Knock yourself out, little girl. I like that bruise of yours." He licked his lips. "Maybe I'll give you another one to match, just for fun."

Lilly beat against the glass to no avail. The cop drove down the lane until they reached a clearing, devoid of neighbors. Lacking any alternative, she planned to throw herself at him, to claw directly for his eyes, as soon as he opened the door.

He exited and circled like a vulture. The cop smiled at her through the window, calm as the night. She wondered how many victims he'd taken here, to this shadowed hollow, to fill his heart with violence.

She tensed, preparing herself.

The door opened and she leapt screaming, fingernails first.

The cop caught her by the throat with the ease of a wide receiver catching a practiced pass. "Naughty, naughty," he tsked, holding her by the windpipe. "Careful, or I might lose my temper."

He threw her to the dirt. His foot introduced itself to her stomach, then to her ribs. He grabbed her hair and dragged her to the front of the car, where he threw her against the hood. He slicked his hair back with one hand, and with the other grabbed her crotch. A sequence of emotions flashed across his face — confusion, revulsion, and finally, white-hot rage. He ripped the mask from her face.

"What the fuck *are* you?"

He slammed his knuckles into her unbruised eye, delivering the matching bruise he'd promised.

Please…

"No tranny scum is going to trap me!"

Another blow, this time to the teeth.

Please…!

"I'll fucking show you…"

Fingers closed around her throat. Everything went white again. She could feel herself disassociating, leaving her body to float skyward like a lightning bug. From above herself, Lilly watched herself dying. Watched herself gasping — "Please!" — as if the bastard would listen.

Something inside her shattered.

No!

No more!

No more begging!

Back on the ground, she forced both eyes open, despite their bruises. The cop hovered above her, both hands to her throat, his face beet red, popping veins and spraying spittle. She thrashed weakly, reaching for the gun at his hip.

"People like you…" the cop grunted, tightening his grip.

By the tips of her fingers, she unclasped the leather loop holding the gun in place. He didn't notice, too pleased at the sight of Lilly's face turning a breathless violet.

"…don't deserve *to exist*."

Blackness gnawed at the edges of her vision. There was no spirit leaving her body, no tunnel of light. Just night and shadow.

With her final burst of strength, she lunged and pulled the gun from its holster. Still holding her throat with both hands, he lifted her head from the hood of the car, preparing to slam her skull into the metal.

Lilly pulled the trigger.

The gunshot split the empty night in two. The bullet did the same thing to the cop's thigh. He stumbled backward, finally freeing her. "I'll kill you!" the beast bellowed. "I'll fucking kill you!"

This time, Lilly took aim. Despite her quivering hands, she struck true.

She sent the bullet deep into the rapist's crotch. He collapsed, jets of blood hemorrhaging from between his legs. He howled at the moon, the life spurting out of him.

Lilly took a step backward, her whole body shaking.

"You'll pay for this…" the cop promised, teeth grit against the pain. "They'll give you life, in a *men's prison…* if you even *make it* to a courtroom…"

She dropped the gun to the dirt. Then she did the only thing she could.

She ran.

And as she ran, she mourned.

She mourned the future at which she would never arrive. She mourned the friendships she would never make and the love she would never know. She mourned her pursuit of happiness cut short by violence. She mourned the ending of her life before it even began, as so many queer youth had mourned before her: a symphony of loss, echoing back through history.

She ran without thought, pushing past the point of failure. What little light guided her came from moonlight and the flickering of fireflies. She didn't know how long she ran. Finally, ahead of her, she blearily beheld the lights of the highway. She made the road and turned northward once again, hoping against all hope that somehow, maybe, just maybe, Rose would still find her.

Maybe everything could somehow still be okay.

A car traveling the other way cut across the highway and rolled to a stop a dozen feet ahead of her.

"Rose?!" Lilly shouted, adrenaline still pumping in her ears.

Red and blue lights flashed atop the car. The police siren screamed to life. So did a voice ordering her down on the ground with her hands behind her head.

She knelt, weeping.

Out beside the highway, the lightning bugs fell back to earth.

RAILROAD BLUES

The rumbling of the train over uneven tracks jostled Ray awake. The first thing he noticed was the headache pulsing behind his eyes. The second thing was the pool of blood spreading across the floor, soaking into the cardboard boxes stacked around the car.

Two of the other stowaways aboard were fighting, clawing and biting and hissing at each other. A third companion — an old-school rambler Ray had crossed paths with more than once, the kind of train-hopper with more tall tales than teeth in his head — lay slumped over, a switchblade sticking out of his gut.

"Holy shit." Ray gripped the neck of his guitar beside him. "Which one of you fuckers killed Roadie?"

"He did!" they both exclaimed.

"So both of you."

"No, him!" they both insisted, continuing to scrap.

Both were dirty, desperate, drug-addled, and wild-eyed. Ray wasn't passing judgement — so was he, after all. But he'd never stabbed an old man in the stomach. One of these fellers did.

"Uh-huh," Ray drawled. "And why'd he kill him, then?"

"He's crazy!" said the one, methamphetamine pockmarks dotting his face like craters.

"He wanted 'is drugs!" said the other, most of his face obscured by a bushy beard that hadn't seen shampoo in all its miserable life. "Roadie said no 'n' he fuckin' stabbed 'im!"

Only one of those seemed like a real motive to Ray.

Roadie, for all his hospitality when it came to sharing meals and stories, was notoriously stingy on the railroad circuit when it came to the subject of substances. And wasn't the pockmarked tramp cleaning his nails with a switchblade before Ray passed out? That would make both motive and means.

He picked up his guitar.

"Life's a lot like hoppin' trains," Roadie had once remarked to Ray. "Rich folks decided which way things was goin' long before you or I got on."

That had always made a lot of sense to Ray. He wondered what Roadie would've had to say if he knew how he was going to die.

Ray swung the guitar at the back of the pockmarked tramp's head. The sound of discordant strings reverberated through the car as he collapsed, unconscious, to the floor.

"Thanks," said the bearded man. "Thought I was next."

Ray regarded his guitar, now splintered and broken. He sighed heavily, then slid open the heavy door. The countryside whipped by at twenty-five outside.

"Come on," Ray said. "Let 'em sort this out at the next stop."

They both leapt from the train, tucking and rolling down the dandelion-dappled hillside. Ray watched the train disappear down the tracks, carrying Roadie's body to the end of the line — that final train station in the sky where all ramblers are someday destined to make their eternal departure.

"See you there someday," Ray muttered, more to himself than to Roadie. "Someday soon, seems more 'n' more like..."

For the first time in a long time, Ray thought about returning home.

As the locomotive vanished into the wastelands, he turned back to the highway, his thumb extended to the oncoming traffic, marching ever onward into the setting sun that glowed like dried blood smeared across the sky.

KEEP YOUR FINGERS CROSSED

Sylvia fussed with the gun concealed beneath her son's letterman jacket as if she was straightening his tie before prom.

"Make sure you stand up straight, so it doesn't bulge out." She took a drag on her cigarette. "You've always had shit posture."

Unlike the other mothers Sylvia knew, she didn't get to dote on her child before prom. Instead of going to the dance, Blake drank cheap whiskey until he threw up and tried heroin for the first time. It would've been the last time too, if she hadn't resuscitated him that night.

That was two years ago. Sylvia had spent them wondering if she should've let him die. Blake spent them wishing she had.

"These things'll kill you," Blake said. He stole the cigarette and took a long drag. "You'd think a doctor oughta know that."

"So will these people if you piss them off," she snapped. "I'm not gonna be there to bail you out this time. If this goes wrong, you need to be ready."

"What do you mean, 'goes wrong?'" Blake buried the tremor in his voice. "I thought you said us and the Wagners were partnering up?"

"Listen to me," Sylvia sighed. Blake had always been so sensitive. "You make deals with devils, you keep your fingers crossed."

Blake finished the cigarette, pouting. Maybe she was right, but Blake would sooner die than admit it.

"Sweetie," she said, bitterly. "Our whole life, we've been on the bottom. Abandoned by your dickhead father to rot away in this shithole. Barely able to keep the lights on, keep you fed, and keep up with the fucking interest on my student loans. Tonight, you do this for *us*. You do this one thing right, and *we'll* be the ones on top."

"He didn't abandon us," Blake muttered. "He OD'd."

"Is there a difference?"

Blake looked to her, the longing for his mother's love visible in his eyes but tainted by resentment and self-loathing. Sylvia drove without glancing away from the road, her hunting rifle suspended in its usual spot in the gun rack over the back window of her pickup. Blake's heart tapped out a nervous rhythm at the thought of the task before him. His right knee bounced to match, sending vibrations through the cabin. Sylvia put a hand on her son's shoulder. He made the mistake of expecting words of comfort.

"Don't fuck it up," she said.

She dropped him off in front of the Wagner Lumberyard, tucked away in the woods beside the 522 outside Haroldston. Her taillights vanished into the darkness. The front gate was unlocked. He was expected.

Blake, a scowling figure with buzzed hair and a former running back's build, put his hands in the pockets of his varsity jacket. Despite the warmth of the night, they were shaking. The lumberyard stood empty, free of the workers that milled about like ants during the day. No witnesses in case anything went wrong. Maybe that was by design.

He headed to the workshop at the back of the compound, just as he'd been instructed. The lights were on inside the workshop.

He took a deep breath then opened the door.

Kurt Wagner was there. So was his younger brother, Eugene. Both brothers sported calloused hands, unruly gray and silver beards, harsh features, and cruel expressions. They hunched over a wooden duck at a table on the left side of the room, Kurt directing Eugene where and how to paint.

Blake's breath caught in his throat at the sight of pistol grips in their waistbands.

He stood up straighter.

"Evenin' boy," Kurt said in a deep, melodic voice. "Step inside."

Blake ducked through the doorframe. Eugene laid his brush down, then came over and shut the door, positioning himself in front of the only exit. Blake glanced around. The workshop was dominated by bladed machinery and elegantly carved wooden ducks, painstakingly painted to create the illusion of life. Moonlight filtered in through sealed windows. On the right end of the room beside an old, rusty table saw, concealed from Blake's previous vantage point, sat a third figure — a sasquatch of a man overflowing from grease-stained overalls, with hands thick enough to crush Blake's windpipe like a wet paper straw.

Blake stared. Sasquatch stared back.

"You like 'em?" Kurt asked.

Blake tore his gaze away. "What?"

"My babies." Kurt gestured to a wooden mallard near the sasquatch. "I took the blue ribbon at the county fair with that beauty here last month."

"Only 'cause I painted him for you," Eugene said, in a voice thinner and whinier than his brother's. "Before that, the best you ever got was honorable mention."

"Hush up now, Eugene," Kurt hissed.

Eugene crossed his arms, sulking. "You know I prefer Gene..."

Blake looked nervously between them. "I thought it was supposed to be jus' you two I was meeting?" His voice cracked like he was still in high school.

Kurt pointed to the sasquatch. "You talkin' about Cousin Artie? Why, he's family. There some kinda problem for me to have my family with me?"

Blake said nothing, scowling. Cousin Artie did the same.

"At the end of the day," Kurt continued, "family's all you really got. Family looks out for each other. Keeps each other safe. Watches each other's backs."

Eugene rolled his eyes, scoffing. Kurt didn't notice. Blake did.

He still didn't say anything.

"I asked you a question, boy," the Wagner patriarch snapped at him. "There some kinda problem I got Cousin Artie here?" His eyes narrowed, but his smile widened. "Why, you weren't planning on tryin' to make some kinda trouble, were you?"

"Course not." Blake shifted his arms, making sure the gun was still concealed.

"Of course not, that's right." Kurt nodded slowly. "You wanna work for me. Help penetrate a younger demographic. That's what your mama told me."

"That's right," Blake nodded.

"I tell you what, last time I had a boy's mama call the lumberyard tryin' to get him a job, I made a point of *not* hirin' him. A man's got to be able to stand on his own two feet."

Blake sucked his teeth. "It ain't like that. Listen, we can hook you up. Lots of kids I know got problems to run from, and nowhere to go."

"And you think your handful of fuckups is the revenue stream I need to take my business to the next level?"

Blake flushed, embarrassed.

"That's just one part of the arrangement," he said. "You know what my mom *does*, right? Think about it. When people can't afford their pain meds no more, she points 'em to me. And all that money'll flow right back into your pocket."

"Oh, I know all about what your mom does."

Kurt suddenly wasn't smiling anymore. Blake didn't like that.

"We know all about it," Eugene repeated. "We ain't idiots."

"We ain't idiots," rumbled Cousin Artie.

"Hush up now, the both of you," Kurt spat at them. Eugene crossed his arms, sulking and glowering. Cousin Artie seemed unfazed. The eldest Wagner turned back to Blake. When he spoke again his voice was as sharp as a table saw.

"Did you think we wouldn't find out?"

"Find out *what*?" Blake's heart throbbed up into his throat. "What are you talking 'bout?"

"Don't play dumb with me," the older brother said.

"I don't think he's playing," the younger brother chuckled.

"I said, *hush up now*," Kurt spat at him. "I won't tell you again, Eugene."

Eugene pouted. "Thought that one was pretty clever…"

Kurt ignored him. "We know your ma's been talkin' to Tremaglio," he said to Blake. "We know she's tryin' to have us cut out of our turf. Our own turf! Why, that's like tryin' to have a family evicted from their home. And you know how I feel about family."

Eugene smiled. "At the end of the day, family's all you—"

Kurt crossed the distance and slapped his brother open-handed across the face. "Hush up now! I said I wouldn't tell you again."

His younger brother stumbled backwards, eyes watering.

"L-L-Look, man," Blake stammered. "I don't know what you're talking about. I don't even *know* nobody named Tremaglio! We just thought—"

"You *just thought*," Kurt interrupted. "That's your problem, ain't it? Thought you could pull a fast one on them dumb ole hillbilly Wagners. But if you're so smart, how come you walked in here *alone*?"

Things were going wrong. He hated it when his mother was right. Blake started running calculations, envisioning options like possible plays to force a first down. He could make a break for it, but Eugene blocked the exit. The windows were all shut, so no diving out that way. He could go for his gun, but the brothers would just go for their own.

Was there no way out?

"We're done here," Kurt said. "Eugene, put him down."

Eugene shot his brother a vicious glare, still rubbing the palm print emblazoned on his cheek. But, like a trained animal, he obeyed anyway, stepping toward Blake as his hand moved toward his gun.

"Woah, woah, woah," Blake protested. "Wait a minute—"

"Hush up now," the younger brother spat. "You made your choices."

"So why don't *you* make your own choices, 'steada always lettin' your brother choose for you?"

Eugene paused, moonlight streaming through the window beside him. Blake took advantage of the newfound opening, pushing through their offense.

"The man won't even give you credit for a damn wooden duck. You think you're ever gonna get anywhere under him?"

"I-It ain't like that," Eugene protested. "It's like Kurt always says, family's all you really g—"

A gunshot ruptured the stillness of the night. The window beside Eugene exploded inward, showering the room in broken glass. The force of a bullet to the temple sent Eugene flailing sideways, blood spurting from the wound. A piece of glass caught Blake above the eye, cutting his eyebrow in two.

Mom?

Kurt, Cousin Artie and Blake all sprang into action simultaneously. Kurt took cover behind his workbench. Cousin Artie lurched forward, bounding toward Blake. And Blake pulled the revolver from his jacket, ducking underneath the sasquatch's clothesline that would've sent him to the floor. He dove behind the tablesaw just in time for Kurt to send a bullet whizzing over his head.

"Gene?!" the older brother wailed, desperate. "Gene, say something!"

Eugene said nothing, quietly staining the floor crimson.

Behind the table saw, Blake flicked the powerswitch. The spinning blade whirred to life. Another bullet flew above his head. Blake peeked out and returned fire, but Kurt ducked back down behind his cover. Blake noted his position.

Cousin Artie spun around, roaring obscenities. He sprinted

toward Blake, the whole workshop shaking with each footfall. Exposing himself, Blake exited cover and ran headfirst toward the charging sasquatch. The beast raised his hands, lunging for Blake's windpipe. Blake feinted like he was going to dodge left, then juked right. The sasquatch fell for it, letting Blake slip through.

Blake stuck his foot out as he passed, tripping the sasquatch. Cousin Artie's weight sent him tumbling forward, off-balance. He tried to catch himself, but it was too late.

His momentum carried him face first into the table saw.

The spinning blade whipped blood and brains around the room, painting long streaks of viscera over the brothers' prize-winning ducks.

Blake stepped forward, revolver pointed ahead with shaking hands.

"You shit-fer-brains little momma's boy," Kurt screamed. "You'll pay for this! You and your whore mother, I swear to God!"

Kurt poked his head back out of cover, in the same place as before. Blake saw the fury and the grief gleaming in his eyes. Then Blake pulled the trigger. Grey matter splattered the back wall of the workshop.

"Hush up now," Blake whispered.

Kurt Wagner obliged, falling silent to the floor.

Quiet fell over the workshop, marred only by the whirring of the table saw. Blake looked around at the three bodies decorating the room: Eugene with a hole in his temple, Kurt with a hole between his eyes, and the sasquatch, his face mutilated beyond recognition.

Blake stepped over Cousin Artie's corpse and cut power to the table saw. He looked down at himself, blood staining his letterman's jacket. He began to cry, tears cutting through the gore splattered across his cheeks. He fell to his knees and wept until he brought himself to emptiness.

His mother was waiting for him outside the lumberyard, leaning against the truck and smoking a cigarette. The hunting rifle sat upright in the backseat, removed from its usual home. She regarded him without affection. He began to cry again.

"Oh sweetie," Sylvia said, pulling the glass from his severed eyebrow. "Shhhh. Shhhh."

She handed him a can of gasoline and a pack of matches.

"Finish it," she said. "And ditch your clothes."

"Not the jacket," he begged. "Please."

"It's covered in blood. That makes it evidence." She took another drag of her cigarette, then blew the smoke in his eyes. "Listen to your mother."

Blake covered Cousin Artie's ruined face with his letterman's jacket, almost an apology, before dousing the room in gasoline. He led a trail of gas outside and dropped a match. The workshop ignited. As his prized memento of his high school victories burned away to ash within, he felt a piece of himself wither away to match.

What had he become?

The lumberyard blazed in their rearview mirror as they drove away. Sylvia glanced sidelong at her son, reduced to only his boxers. He watched the darkness passing by with hollow eyes.

"Maybe you can't see it yet," she said. "But you done somethin' real good here tonight. From here on out, you and I are gonna *run* this town. I'm…" She paused, almost reluctant to say it. "I'm proud of you."

"Please," Blake croaked. "Don't ever make me do nothin' like that again."

"Of course, sweetie. You'll never have to, ever again. I promise."

Beside the steering wheel, Sylvia kept her fingers crossed.

ONCE I WAS STONED

Raymond Reynolds sat in his battered old Bronco in the lot behind the Detweiler County courthouse, burning down a joint.

Whenever a bailiff appeared out the back door, usually to take a smoke break of their own, he hid by reclining and slinking down into the seat. Not like that would do anything for the smell, but this wasn't Ray's first rodeo. He kept a classic example of stoner ingenuity beneath his passenger seat: a paper towel tube stuffed with scented dryer sheets, a sort of poor man's air purifier.

Mmm. He blew a lungful of pungent marijuana smoke through the tube, hacking up his guts. *Now that's outdoor fresh.*

The joint dead, and his head pleasantly abuzz, he went through his usual routine of popping a breath mint, applying a fresh layer of cheap cologne, and drowning his eyes in a generous flood of Visine.

He circled around front and clickclacked up the long marble steps in his heavy black cowboy boots, adjusting the wide brim of his flat-top Stetson as he climbed. Milton, one of the sheriff's boys, was manning the metal detector at the front door.

"Mornin' Ray," he drawled.

"Milton, how do? I went ahead and already left all the explosives'n whatnot back in the truck." Ray emptied his pockets into the waiting bin: wallet, keys, roach, pen — *wait, no, not the roach!* — pocket knife, reporter's notebook. The sheriff's deputy leaned in closer than Ray would've preferred, eyeing him intently. "Was just a joke, Milton, that's all…"

"You, uh, you feelin' alright there, Ray?"

Oh God. He knows. Ray's heart beat a paranoid rhythm against his ribcage. He cleared his throat, not too nervously, he hoped.

"Yeah, fine," is what he said. "Why d'ya ask?"

"It's just that, well, frankly…"

Gig's over. Ship's going down. Sweat beaded across Ray's forehead. *It was a good run. Guess I'm not cut out to be no public servant.*

"It just looks like you been cryin', is all?" Milton said, almost embarrassed.

"…crying?"

Ray touched his face. The eye drops. *You moron. You absolute idiot. Think of something to say. Do it!* Jesus, had his mouth stopped working? Just open the lips and form the words…

"Yeah, I was, uh…" Inspiration hit him like a freight train. "I was just listenin' to a bit of the ole Hank Williams back in my truck." He wiped his eyes and affected a warble in his throat. "He just always gets me, y'know?"

Milton nodded solemnly. "Me too, man." He patted Ray's shoulder. "Me too."

Bullet successfully dodged, Ray collected his things and stepped inside the courthouse. In stark contrast to the handsome exterior of wind-polished marble, the inside resembled the set of a cheap horror movie. The broken tiles, flickering lights and stains of unknown age and origin on the walls and floors were complemented by the shuffling of a line of correctional facility residents in orange jumpsuits, several of whom Ray recognized from high school.

He slunk through the third door on the left, the Office of the Prothonotary — a term he had to have his editor define for him his first day on the job. "Clerk of courts," turns out it meant. Why they didn't just *say that* was one of the obscure quirks of the legal system that Ray didn't think he'd ever grasp.

Brenda Fischer, duly elected keeper of legal records for Detweiler County, Pennsylvania, sat in her usual spot on the far side of a cheap linoleum counter, flipping through a file, separated from the office lobby by a pane of glass with a slot for paperwork. Ray figured someone must've tried jumping the counter at some point, prompting the county to install the divider. But there was a part of him that still thought it looked strange: a physical barrier between the public and the public record, protected by a middle aged gatekeeper in pearl earrings and floral print.

"Howdy," Ray said as he sauntered up to the counter. "What's good today?"

"God," Brenda said, unironically.

"Uh-huh, all the time," Ray concurred, tongue somewhere in his cheek.

Brenda closed her eyes and raised a hand skyward. "He put a song of praise in this heart of mine."

"I always liked that song… But when I said what's good, I meant, like, crime and such?"

"Well," Brenda shook her head. "I wouldn't say there's anything *good* there."

"How about anything *interesting*?"

Maybe Ray's pot-muddled brain was just inventing things, but he thought he caught a flash of mischievousness in her eyes. Then he blinked and it was gone.

"How interestin' it is, I don't know, but I did go ahead and set this aside for you." She produced a file held shut by a rubber band. "Some new filings in the case 'tween the Fultons and the Davidsons."

These two farming families had been at odds for generations for reasons no one quite remembered anymore. The latest flare-up in the feud involved back-and-forth graffitiing, stolen livestock, and a series of increasingly graphic bestiality-related rumors, which had all culminated in a lawsuit alleging "defamation of character and intentional infliction of emotional distress." Ray was still learning, but he'd picked up enough to know this was basically legal talk for "saying mean things about someone."

"Welp," Ray said, taking the file from the slot in the glass, "that oughta keep the ole editor off my back for another day." He gave a sort of half-assed salute.

Brenda smiled. "Have fun now." Ray caught another glimpse of some sort of hidden meaning, this time being, like, *pretty sure* he wasn't just imagining it.

"You too, man," Ray said.

He read through the documents back at the newsroom, a converted storefront on Second Street with *The Haroldston Herald* printed in faded gothic lettering on the fogged glass door. Inside was crammed with more desks than actual reporters, remnants of the paper's glory days, already years gone before Ray had ever ended up on staff.

Why his editor Deandre had decided he should be responsible for covering crime, courts and local government eluded him. His head swam trying to decipher the dense legalese of the Fulton-Davidson filings. Motions to deny discovery requests, arguments about privilege and relevance… Wait, what was this?

Stuck into the center of one of the filings was a letter printed on official county letterhead. He looked at the previous page, which cut off part way through a sentence. On the page after the letter, the sentence continued. Whatever this was, it wasn't supposed to be here. *Unless…* Ray remembered Brenda's funny smile.

"Judge Holder," the letter began. "It has come to my attention that you have removed several documents from the public file of *Davidson v. Fulton* and its related countersuit."

It was about that point Ray realized that what he was holding, was *news*.

Taking the folder with him, he ducked into the back alley for a smoke break. He took a joint from his pocket and lit up, and let it dangle from the corner of his mouth, taking drags as he read, knowing he'd just had his entire evening blown up.

The letter continued: "Although you had indeed previously stricken the motions removed from the record, only items that are formally expunged are no longer accessible via the public file, as you are doubtlessly aware given your extensive legal credentialing."

Interesting shit. He flicked bits of ash from the letter, leaking smoke from the opposite corner of his mouth as the joint. *So the judge musta had some kinda personal reason for yoinking those documents.*

Lo and behold: "Furthermore, given the fact that all the motions that you have removed from the public file concern Mr. Fulton and his legal counsel's attempts to recuse you from this case over allegations of personal bias, I am deeply concerned, as you should be, about the obvious appearance of impropriety."

Ray held the joint at arm's length down the alley and poked his head back through the door into the newsroom. "Hey! Dee!" he hollered for his editor.

Her tough, husky voice answered from her office around the corner. "What!"

"What's re-cuse mean?"

"What?!"

"What does," Ray hollered, louder, "*recuse* mean?"

"Take someone off a case! 'Cause they can't be trusted to do their job right!"

"Okay, thanks," starting to shut the door.

"Hol' up, why you ask? You got news?"

"Working on it!" Ray answered. "Give me the afternoon."

He closed the door and continued reading.

"I fear that, should these documents not be returned to their proper place, I will be required to escalate these concerns beyond a simple letter, such as to the Judicial Conduct Board. I would see them in place within the week."

Signed, Brenda M. Fischer, Prothonotary, Detweiler County, Pennsylvania. Ray checked the date up top. It was sent almost two weeks ago. Looked like Brenda was escalating.

Brenda, you son of a bitch. He killed the joint, nodding

appreciatively. *...Wait, that doesn't work. Brenda, you... bitch? Wait, no, that's worse...*

Back inside, Ray googled the Judicial Conduct Board and found a number for an office in Harrisburg. It rang through to voicemail. He left a message with his number and email, explaining he was a reporter working on a story, then sat drumming his fingers on his desk, pondering his next move.

More than anything else, he needed two things: copies of the motions that had been removed from the public file, and, ideally, a response on the record from Judge Holder. Though Ray suspected the judge would, as they say in the business, "decline to comment," which would probably have to do.

Now Ray was none too thrilled at the prospect of approaching the judge, an immense man twice Ray's height and width, with a voice as sharp as a striking gavel, and accusing him of mishandling documents, and probably worse. So it was out of procrastination as much as practicality that Ray put off talking to Judge Holder, at least until he'd had the chance to figure out why the Fultons wanted the judge kicked off their case. And for that, Ray would need to talk to Franklin Conway, the attorney who had filed the missing motions.

He hopped back in the Bronco, lit up another joint, and drove on over to the converted rancher on Matilda Avenue that housed the law practice of Franklin & Conway. He ended up circling the block three times, convinced the house had somehow just *vanished*, which at least gave him time to burn the joint down to the roach before he finally found the place, exactly where it'd always been.

The receptionist at the front desk sniffed the air and wrinkled her nose at Ray's approach. She called for her boss like she expected him to kick Ray out. Instead, Franklin Conway, a wiry figure only a few years older than Ray, wearing a three-piece suit certainly worth more than the trade-in value of his Bronco, invited Ray back to his office. The converted bedroom was dominated by bookshelves sagging under the weight of doorstoppers with funny names like "The

Law of Lawyering," which seemed redundant to Ray, but what did he know?

"Mr. Reynolds," Conway gestured to a plush chair on one side of a handsome mahogany desk. "A pleasure that you've finally made a house call to our humble practice."

Ray plunked himself down into the cushions. "Humble as the Apostle Paul," he said, eyeing a crystal bowl filled with Werther's caramels.

"Could I offer you a candy?"

"Wouldn't want to impose," Ray muttered, already scooping out as many as he could. He stuffed a fistful into his pocket.

"Please, help yourself." Conway frowned, watching Ray return for a second handful. "So what can…" The reporter continued scooping caramels. "Mr. Reynolds, what can…"

Ray stuffed the second handful into his other pocket and went back for a third.

Conway pulled the dish out of his reach.

"So," the lawyer said, more firmly, "what can I do for you today, Mr. Reynolds?"

"Oh right, I, um, I got something I've been meaning to ask you."

"Which is?"

Ray unwrapped a candy and tossed it into his mouth. "Well, it's like, the name of your firm? Franklin, *and* Conway? Isn't the last name usually enough? Or did you just want to double down?"

"Right, right, yes," the attorney chuckled. "I should've guessed."

"Bet you get this a lot," Ray said around his caramel.

"You saw how, on the door, it says Franklin and Conway?"

"Uh-huh."

"Perhaps it escaped your doubtlessly impeccable perception, but underneath that, it also says 'Albert *Franklin* and Franklin *Conway*, Attorneys at Law."

"Is one of those, like, your pen name?"

Conway sighed. Ray smiled to himself.

"Let me ask *you* a question instead, Mr. Reynolds."

"Alright, shoot."

"You're fairly new to the comings-and-goings around here?"

"I'm *from* here, man," Ray said.

"I mean, in the *legal* community here. Movers. Shakers. Et cetera. You've been on this beat, how long, a year?"

"Next month."

"And what newspaper were you at before?"

"Um…"

"As I thought. Well, my partner, Albert, handles estate law and the like — the sort of thing less likely to sell newspaper subscriptions than certain matters to which I attend, perhaps, but a service that is no less vital to this community."

"You mean to your 'mover' and your 'shaker' friends?"

"Mr. Reynolds, we're on the same side here."

"That so?"

"We're both public servants, in our own ways. Both of us in search of some truth, either in the courtroom or the court of public opinion. Either way, we do much the same work: present the facts and encourage appropriate judgment."

"All I do's report the shit, man. I don't get paid enough to encourage judgment."

"You're a paragon of objectivity, I have no doubt." Conway smiled in a practiced manner, his pearly white teeth gleaming behind steepled fingertips. "So, once more, what can I do for you today, Mr. Reynolds?"

"I'm workin' on another story 'bout the Fulton-Davidson case," Ray finally cut to the chase.

"Yes, you've been quite… *attentive*. That hasn't gone unappreciated."

"Yeah, yeah," Ray waved his hand, as if swatting away gnats. "Thing is, I was looking over some of the recent filings down at the courthouse, and it seems like some of them are, like, *missing* or something?"

The attorney's smile widened. "Is that so? I can't say I would know why…"

"Oh, I'm working on that one." Ray winked. "I was just hoping you might have a spare copy you could lend me?"

"Now that you mention it…" As if he'd been waiting for an opportunity, Conway opened his topmost desk drawer and removed a packet of papers. "I have one right here." He slid them over across the desktop.

"Thank you kindly," Ray said, taking them. "Want to offer any comment?"

Conway shook his head, chuckling. "I'm sure you'll find the filing speaks for itself."

"Right then." Ray lifted himself from the chair and turned to leave. "Fair winds, following seas, all that…"

"Good day, Mr. Reynolds. Oh, and one more thing…" The reporter turned back toward the lawyer. "If you ever find yourself in need of legal representation, you feel free to give me a call."

"…for what?"

He sniffed the air. "I think we both know. Now, on your way."

"Uh-huh, you too, man," he muttered, already leaving.

He read through the motion to recuse in his truck in the parking lot, smoking another joint. In an accidental moment of self-reflection, he almost wondered if he should ease up on his stash, maybe try not to smoke it all before payday, but he got distracted by the allegations Conway had made in his filing.

Seems that Holder, first elected all the way back in 1992, had once been an unexpected outsider candidate for a seat on the county bench. His original campaign, according to the campaign finance reports Conway had attached to his motion, was funded in large part by rather generous donations from one Josiah Davidson – now a plaintiff in the defamation of character lawsuit that Judge Holder currently oversaw. According to Conway's argument, and Ray could follow his logic, the fact that Holder owed his job to the Davidson family meant he was incapable of delivering a fair judgment in a case where Josiah Davidson himself stood to make a pretty penny in damages.

Holder had not only denied the motion, he ordered it struck from the record, then went ahead and took the copies that were supposed to remain on file down in the Office of the Prothonotary. For good measure, Ray assumed. Seemed to him, though, that Holder had caused himself more trouble than if he'd just denied the motion and left it there. Trying to get rid of the file from the public record was the sure sound of a guilty dog barking if Ray had ever heard one.

He smiled, taking a final pull off the joint. The story was starting to come together. But he couldn't put off talking to the big man forever. Ray groaned, then rolled another funny cigarette for the trek back across town to the courthouse.

Ray had just parked when his phone rang. The screen showed a 717 number he almost recognized. He still had half his joint left. He licked his fingers, pinched the cherry, and answered the call.

"Um, hello?"

"Mr. Reynolds?" came a deep, heavy voice.

"Who's asking?"

"Justice Marlon Kristoff," the voice answered with a touch of annoyance. "With the Judicial Conduct Board."

"Oh, right, thanks for calling me back. I'm working on this story about a Judge Robert Holder down here in Detweiler County. Could you tell me if there's been any, like, complaints, or investigations or whatever?"

"No."

Ray waited for him to say more, but nothing came.

"Like… no, there hasn't? Or no, you can't tell me?"

"The latter. I can neither confirm nor deny any specific reports or investigations."

"Um, okay… Why not?"

"It's simple." Ray detected a familiar condescension in his tone. "To protect the integrity of the reporting system, all complaints and subsequent inquiries remain strictly confidential. Having these matters sensationalized in the press would only serve to undermine public confidence in the judiciary."

"Wait. Let me get this straight." Ray rubbed his temples. "You keep all the shady shit that judges get up to… hidden from the public… because you think that makes you look… more trustworthy? To the public? Am I missing something?"

"Many things," the voice sighed. "But I'm a busy man, and lack the time to explain them to you. Best of luck with your story, Mr. Reynolds."

"Uh-huh," Ray grumbled. "You too, man."

Ray sat in his truck, angry-smoking the rest of his joint, thinking how it was awfully convenient that what was best for "maintaining public confidence in the judiciary" was also best for keeping those same folks in power. Go fuckin' figure.

On the second floor of the courthouse hung a printout of the day's schedule: what cases were being heard by whom, at what time, and in which courtroom. The tiny letters stubbornly squirmed and rearranged themselves as Ray tried to read them. He stood there for a good ten minutes, squinting and rubbing his bloodshot eyes, before they began to make sense.

Judge Holder was overseeing a hearing scheduled until 3:30, with a fifteen-minute break before another obligation. Now Ray happened to know, from his experience observing the backdoor of the courthouse while toking up in his truck, that Judge Holder was a prolific smoker, able to chain smoke three cancer sticks in the time it took a normal fella to smoke one. Which Ray figured, being himself more than a little familiar with the compulsive mechanics of addiction, meant that Judge Holder would spend those precious few free minutes sucking down smoke out back.

Ray posted up around the corner from the back door. Sure enough, shortly after the church bells tolled half past three, Judge Holder emerged through the doorway, an enormous man in his long black judicial robes with a head of thinning hair halfway from blonde to gray. Ray fumigated himself in bodyspray and waited until the judge's cigarette was lit before launching his ambush.

"Judge Holder," Ray slid into place, seemingly out of nowhere. "How do?"

"Reynolds," the judge groaned.

"Enjoying a smoke break?"

Holder looked at him with beady blue eyes, folded in the thick contours of his heavy face. "Not anymore."

Ray squinted, the obvious insult whistling as it went over his head. *He's obviously still smoking, what could he mean?* The judge cleared his throat after Ray, not really realizing it, had stood staring at him for several seconds.

"Do you *want* something?" He angled the pack of Marlboros at Ray. "Cowboy Killer?"

"Nah thanks," Ray chuckled. "I don't smoke." And before Holder could respond, he jumped right into it: "So I'm working on this story about the Fulton-Davidson case?"

"I'm sure you are," Holder said.

In one astonishing breath, the judge burned the cigarette halfway down to the filter and exhaled a cloud of smoke so massive that Ray momentarily forgot what he was doing as he watched it twist and float away on the afternoon breeze.

"Well, as pleasant as this has been…" Holder said, waving him away.

"Oh right," Ray remembered. "So the thing is, I'm hoping you could comment on why you removed the Fultons' motion to recuse from the public record?"

Instantly, the judge's whole body tightened. Ray could practically see the calculations unfolding behind his squinting eyes.

"That motion was struck from the record," Holder responded, obviously off-balance. From the way he grimaced afterwards, Ray guessed he regretted answering at all.

"Now I ain't a lawyer," the reporter smiled, "but don't they gotta be, uh, *explunged* if they're gonna be taken outta the public record though?"

"Look, Reynolds," the judge growled, and killed the second half of his cigarette in a single breath. "I'm afraid I can't comment on pending cases."

And before Ray could respond, he flicked the cigarette butt to the asphalt, swiped his keycard to unlock the back door, and rushed back inside, pulling the door closed behind him. Which was fine enough with Ray. He'd gotten what he needed.

Ray spent the next hour in his truck, typing up a first stab at the story on his laptop and burning down yet another joint. When five o'clock rolled around, and courthouse staff would soon be making their exit for the day, Ray left his vehicle and circled around front of the building. He stood leaning against a marble pillar as lawyers and administrators trickled out the doors.

He remembered all at once, in one of those strange spasms of memory that send something presumed forgotten floating back into mind, his first impression of this very courthouse from back when he was a kid. He was pretty sure his parents had gotten a DUI, which seemed on brand, and had been unable to make arrangements for little Ray the day of their hearing. He didn't remember much of the proceedings themselves, but he had been awed by the solemn marble building, thinking it must need such strong pillars to uphold the heavy weight of justice.

What a fuckin' idiot.

Ray was in the middle of giggling profusely at all this, caught in a self-sustaining fit of pothead hysteria, when Brenda Fischer emerged from the courthouse. She gave him a calculating scowl.

"Hey Brenda," he giggled.

"Raymond," she nodded. "You okay?"

"Oh sure, just havin' fun, like you told me."

She smiled. "Well, I'm glad." She started off down the steps.

Ray forcibly swallowed the last of his laughter. "Was hopin' to talk to you a minute?"

"I'm sure," she said back over her shoulder. "I'm off the clock, though?"

"Right…"

She made the sidewalk, then stopped. "Public sidewalk though, you know. Can't control where you decide to walk while I'm headin' home."

She started walking again, more slowly. Ray jogged on his stubby legs down the steps to catch up, wondering how he was so out of shape.

"So, can," he huffed, "can I, y'know, ask you a question?"

She side-eyed him. "This on the record?"

"Yours or mine?"

"Well," Brenda looked around. "We ain't in a courtroom."

"And," Ray raised empty hands, "I ain't taking notes."

"I see that now."

"So what's the deal with that letter, huh?"

Brenda smiled. "Letter? Darn! I knew I had *misplaced* a copy somewhere…"

"Uh-huh, yeah man, things get misplaced all the time, I feel you. But, like, let's just say *if* you *had* done it on purpose…?"

"Then you're asking why?"

"Well, I think I got the who, the what, the where, and so on…" Ray shrugged. "So, yeah, I guess I'm asking why."

"Because it was the right thing to do?" Brenda said, self-evidently. "Besides, Raymond, in a way, aren't we in the same business?"

"And what business is that?"

"Providing the public with a record," she said, nodding solemnly. "They deserve one, don't they?"

"Brenda," Ray laughed. "You son of a bitch."

"*Excuse* me?"

"No! Like as a compliment! Like, 'ahhh! You son of a bitch!'" Ray could tell from the way she'd crossed her arms, tapping her foot against the pavement, that he wasn't helping his case. "Look, I'm sorry, I'm just gonna stop talkin'…"

She sighed. "Listen, Raymond, you're good people." She placed a hand on his shoulder. "But you need Jesus."

"So I've been told."

"You know, my church is always welcoming new members." She said it with the tone of a salesman before a practiced pitch.

"Oh man, um, would you look at the time!" Ray brought up and pointed to his wrist before realizing he wasn't wearing a watch — didn't even *own* one, as a matter of fact. "Almost press time! Headlines and deadlines ain't so different from time and tide — they wait for no man."

"Alright, alright, no need for the song and dance," Brenda scoffed. "Don't worry. I'll pray for you."

"Uh-huh," Ray called over his shoulder, already leaving. "You too, man!"

Though he did wonder, walking back to the courthouse lot, if Jesus could turn water into wine, could he turn weeds into, y'know… *weed*? Dandelions into marijuana, now *that* would be a miracle. Ray was so lost in this train of thought as he reached his truck that he remained completely oblivious to Judge Holder as the judge emerged from a nearby alley, camouflaged in its shadows in his solemn black suit.

"Reynolds," the judge intoned, approaching.

"Holy *shit*!" Ray damn near jumped out of his skin. "Where'd you come from?"

Holder ignored his question. "I take it you plan to pursue your story?"

"Well, uh, yeah," the reporter stammered, trying to regain his cool. "And I made sure to give you a chance to participate."

Holder placed a hand to his own chest, as if Ray had wounded him. "But your chance was no chance at all, son. Judges ain't allowed to comment on legal proceedings outside of the courtroom."

"Well," Ray shrugged. "I'll be sure to note that in the story."

"You got me like a sitting duck here. That ain't fair."

"I'm real sorry about that, but I got a job to do."

"Yes." From inside his robes, Holder produced a manila folder. "And part of that job is to consider your sources." He handed the folder to Ray.

"And what's this?"

"Proof that Ms. Fischer's little crusade isn't the act of public altruism she's convinced you of."

Ray opened it. Inside were court records from a DUI case just under four years ago. A drunk driver, already speeding, had failed to slow down in a school zone, and struck a young boy, killing him. Holder had sentenced the driver to ten years behind bars for manslaughter. The driver, whose mugshot bore a striking familial resemblance to his sister, was one Jeremy Fischer.

"Uh-huh, okay, right…" Ray scratched his chin.

"Brenda's younger brother ended an innocent life, you understand?" Holder's eyes were wide and intense under his heavy brows. "I had no choice but to sentence him to prison." He hung his head, slumping his broad shoulders. "To make the *just* decision… it is a heavy burden to bear, sometimes."

Yeah, yeah. Get off the cross, we need the wood. Ray sniffed and rubbed his nose. *Shoulda probably seen somethin' like this comin'.*

Ray cleared his throat. "So, uh, where're you goin' with this, exactly?"

"Isn't it obvious?" Holder took a step closer, dwarfing the reporter. "The woman's let her emotions cloud her professional judgement. I'm up for my retention vote next year, you see. And Brenda, she's been biding her time, planning to find some way to stir up trouble for me, get even at me for what I *had* to do to her brother."

"That so?"

"Don't forget, son, *her* reelection campaign is coming up too. And here she is, trying to dust up a scandal for someone else, keep the voters' attention where she wants it. The way I see it," Holder laid a hand on his shoulder, "you have a huge story by the tail here, son."

"Yeah, man," Ray smiled, hoping the judge couldn't smell the pot scent leaking out from his truck. "Starting to think I just might."

"You have a corrupt prothonotary overstepping her authority to try to run the courthouse according to her will." Holder gripped his shoulder, tighter than was comfortable. "That's an incredible scoop for you."

"Sure, man, sure." Ray let his upper body go limp and sort of slunk away from Holder's grip. "That's just an awfully *convenient* way for you to see this story, is all, you know?"

"Careful, son."

"And stop calling me that? Okay?"

Holder raised a confused eyebrow, as if surprised that Ray, dirty no-account stoner that he admittedly was, wasn't just folding like a gambler with a bad poker hand.

"It's like," Ray continued, "you're doing exactly the same thing that got you in hot water to begin with. Tryna hide shit from the public? You see that, right?"

"Can you not see how she's trying to manipulate you?"

Ray laughed. "So what's all this you're doin', then?"

"My boy, I'm trying to *help* you."

"Oh wow," Ray clapped his hands to his face in mock amazement, "and what helps me also has you come out lookin' good, well golly gee, ain't that just something."

"Reynolds." The judge's expression darkened like a summer sky shrouded in storm clouds. He adopted an angry, restrained hush to his voice. He shook his head slowly. "I'm disappointed in you."

Ray laughed in his face. "Right? Me too, man. But you ain't my boss and you ain't family, so I can't rightly say I care. Now, if you'll excuse me, I got a story to file."

He ducked into his vehicle with all the speed and none of the grace of an Olympian, racing to keep the pot stench from escaping. He watched his rearview mirror as he rolled away. Judge Holder stood watching him go, anger smoldering in his eyes like coals in a dying fire.

Ray waited until he turned the corner to light a joint.

The story ran across the front page of the next day's issue of The

Haroldston Herald. Ray wasn't sure what he was expecting to happen, maybe the phone to ring off the hook, or a flood of emails from concerned readers. Neither came. "Don't take it personally, kid," his editor told him. It felt hard not to.

But, two days later, a handwritten letter to the editor written in looping cursive turned up in the newspaper's mailbox. It was sent by Evelyn Harolds, chair of the Detweiler County Historical Society.

"Hey, Dee!" he hollered.

"What?" his editor hollered back from her office.

"We got a letter to the editor!"

"We did?"

"Like an actual, snail mail letter!"

"What's it say?"

Ray opened the envelope and read quietly.

"What's happening in the courthouse is nothing new," the letter began. "Maybe not too many remember, or care to remember, how our county's first president judge, Albert Detweiler, was kicked out of office by the state legislature for blatant disregard of the Abolition Act of 1780, taking bribes from southern industry to send freedmen back to bondage."

Ray blinked and held the letter closer to his face.

"Somewhat more well remembered is the story of how in 1927, the body of District Attorney Ned DuBois washed up on the banks of the Juniata. A pair of federal agents sent to investigate found ties to a bootlegging racket in Philadelphia, before they also showed up a hundred miles downriver, full of bullet holes."

Ray whistled, almost impressed.

"Maybe removing some files isn't so bad as all that," the letter concluded. "But maybe it's time we start demanding better of the men who claim to be good enough to judge us."

Ray cleared his throat. "I'll just let you read it yourself," he hollered.

Outside of that letter, nothing much seemed to happen. If the Judicial Conduct Board made any kind of ruling on Judge Holder's involvement in the Fulton-Davidson case, Ray sure as hell couldn't tell. The case dragged on, the attorneys arguing back and forth in their head-spinning jargon. Judge Holder continued to sit at his throne on the bench, more-or-less ignoring Ray except to toss him bitter, reproachful glares in the courthouse halls. And Ray continued on in his usual way, getting more stoned than the Apostle Paul.

Some weeks on, Ray was enjoying a customary midafternoon smoke break in the courthouse parking lot, listening to Hank Williams and feeling vaguely sorry for himself for any number of reasons, when someone came rapping on his window. Ray yelped and flailed wildly, trying in vain to hide his joint and bag of weed from whoever had just busted him.

Brenda Fischer was on the other side of his window. She motioned for him to roll it down. He shook his head. She motioned again, more insistently. He did so, grimacing.

"Bren*nnn*da," he said. "So, uh, this is *not* what it looks like."

She rolled her eyes. "Come off it, Raymond. In fact…" She reached in, plucked the joint from his hand, and took a drag long enough to leave her sputtering and coughing.

Ray took the joint back, jaw limp in amazement. "*What* is happening right now?"

"Here." She tossed a paper in his lap. "You'll understand."

Ray squinted at the page. It was a letter from Judge Holder to the president judge of the county. Apparently, Holder no longer intended to seek retention and would be stepping down from the upcoming election.

Huh. No shit.

At first, Ray wondered if he had managed to do some good for once, but a sentence at the end of the letter made his smile disappear faster than shit moves through a goose: "I also look forward to continuing my service to the legal community as a newly appointed member of the Judicial Conduct Board of Pennsylvania."

Ray dropped the letter.

Everything that happened, and Holder just goes to work for the same folks who were supposed to keep him on the straight and narrow? Go fucking figure. Just one more in a long line of backroom deals struck between people *with* power out of sight, out of mind, and out of reach of all the people *without* it: the unwashed masses, the ramblers and the vagabonds, and the whole damn world of working class schmucks with all their blue collar blues. Ray sputtered like a dying engine.

"Mother*fucker*…"

"You know I don't approve of such vulgar language," Brenda nodded, blushing. "But you said it."

"I can't believe it."

She sighed. "Well, I can."

"You, uh…" Ray gestured to his passenger seat, more out of politeness than anything. "You wanna burn one down?"

"No, I don't think so," she said, blinking rapidly. She rubbed her eyes. "Probably shouldn't've done it at all." She shook her head. "It's just… I…I, uh… " She trailed off sadly.

"It's okay. I get it." Ray passed her the eyedrops from his center console. "Here. It'll help."

She took the little bottle. "Thanks, Raymond." She turned to leave, but hesitated. "And this was all… off the record, right?"

"Shit," he laughed. "I was gonna ask you the same thing."

Brenda nodded and turned to leave, but Ray stopped her.

"Hey Brenda, um, I just wanted to say…" He wanted to offer condolences for her brother, couldn't figure out how to put it, and then sat staring at her, not realizing he'd trailed off.

"Well?" she finally said.

"Wha?"

"What?"

"Uh-huh," Ray said. "You too, man."

Brenda blinked. Then she laughed, a rollicking belly laugh bigger than any he'd ever heard from her. "You really do need Jesus," Brenda wheezed, turning to leave. She tilted back her head and doused her eyes as she walked away. Ray watched her go, his smile melting into a long, sad scowl.

He sat there and finished his joint, figuring ole brother Hank Williams might've had it right all along. No need to worry, no use in trying or striving, 'cause nothin' ever works out anyway. But when the song was over, what choice did Ray have, did anyone have, but to keep striving? For *what*, he didn't know…

Ray checked the clock. He should probably be getting back to work.

Instead, he turned up the volume and rolled another joint.

THE INTERNSHIP

Cera Dieben strained against the plastic restraints digging into her wrists.

Seeping through the cement ceiling, she could still hear the yammering of drunken tourists feeding the casino their hard-earned cash. A slender young woman with strawberry blonde hair and serious hazel eyes, she'd been living off tourists' pocket money, supposedly working an internship she'd stopped attending and dreading leaving Las Vegas to return for her junior year at UCLA. *This* was where she felt alive.

Well, not "this" exactly, zip-tied to a wooden chair in a casino basement…

Working a gambling floor was supposed to be a step up from pickpocketing. When her friend Lucy had passed along the tip that Shady J was putting together a card-counting crew, Cera was happy to serve as lookout, provided she got paid. Now she was waiting for the pit boss to come smack her head against the concrete a couple times to teach her a lesson.

For years, Cera had survived thanks to an uncanny ability to remain indistinct and invisible, even while emptying someone's pockets in broad daylight. It was how she earned her living. So there was *no way* she got spotted. Not a doubt in her mind — she got sold out. Guess that's why you don't take jobs from people *literally* named "Shady."

Her wrists burned from pulling against the plastic. No way she could break them. The chair, on the other hand, was a rickety wooden frame well past its prime.

She placed her feet firmly against the concrete.

It had all happened so quickly. "Gotta take a wicked piss," Shady J had excused himself from the table, disappearing toward the men's room. Next thing she knew, a pair of floormen grabbed her by the arms and dragged her away from her post. From the commotion behind her, it sounded like the rest of the crew had gotten pinched too.

Shady J had sold the whole lot of them down the river.

Cera's brain raced like a pit car in need of a tune up. She could still make it out of this, right? She'd managed to make it out of everything else she'd ever gotten into. Sure, the odds were stacked against her, but then again, weren't they always? Vegas, baby!

She took a deep breath before pushing off with all her strength, sending the chair clattering to the concrete. The cheap wood splintered beneath her. Cera lay there groaning, new bruises already forming. A splintered piece of armrest still remained tied to one wrist, but at least she could move freely again.

The elevator dinged.

"Shit!"

She sprinted for an oversized fern blooming from an ornate pot beside the elevator.

The elevator doors started to open.

Cera leapt behind the pot just in time. Out of the elevator stepped a veritable bulldog in a pinstriped suit, all fat and muscle and jowls. Cera stretched out her free hand from behind cover, her fingers straining for the employee keycard dangling from his belt.

Come on, just a little further...

By the tips of her fingers, she slipped the keycard from its holder as he passed. Cera slipped out from behind the fern and into the waiting elevator, where she swiped the card. As the buttons illuminated, the bulldog's growls sounded behind her. Cera punched the button for the ground floor.

"What the fuck…?" The pit boss appraised the empty, broken chair, then spun around with unexpected grace. His eyes narrowed at the sight of Cera in the elevator with his keycard. "Oh *hell* no!"

The bulldog began bounding toward her, jowls flapping as he ran. Cera pounded the 'close doors' button. The elevator doors began sliding slowly into place, twin glaciers inching together.

She kept slapping the button. "Come on! Doors together… door together…"

The floor shook beneath the bulldog's heavy footfalls. With each quake, he grew closer to his quarry. Cera adopted a new tactic of holding the button down entirely.

"Doors *fucking* together! Who makes these things?!"

Abandoning the button, she turned her attention to the wooden rod still fastened to her left wrist. With a grunt, she ripped it free from the plastic.

The bulldog reached the elevator. "Hold it," he barked.

He placed one fat hand on either side, forcing them to reverse.

"Elevator's full," Cera answered.

Wielding the splintered wood like a rapier, she brought the jagged end upwards in a sharp arc, catching the bulldog in the face. He stumbled backwards, bleeding. She jabbed him hard in the belly, forcing him back outside, then jammed the stick into the button so hard it sparked. The doors finally closed.

"Try the stairs."

● ● ●

Thankfully, the elevator got her to the ground floor before the bulldog could catch up. She bolted for the nearest exit, knocking over slow-shuffling tourists in the process, and took refuge in her favorite cantina across the way. The bartender gave her a familiar nod. Cera, still only twenty, slipped a twenty into the tip jar. He conveniently forgot to ask for ID.

Over a frozen margarita, she mulled her situation.

She'd only been here a month, and this was already the second time she'd found herself in deep shit. She got lucky the first time — the living room incident — but that was only because Lucy had been there to save her ass. Not that she'd ever admit that to Lucy.

They'd met as freshmen at UCLA, both with plans to study economics and become high-powered career women. You know what they say about best-laid plans? Now, two years later, Lucy had dropped out to become a call girl. Cera was only supposed to be in the city for her internship — *unpaid*, of course — with a labor forecasting firm located off the strip. Instead, she'd mostly spent her days pickpocketing tourists and getting tanked.

Lucy had been the one to suggest she talk to Shady J. One of her regular clients, Shady J was a gambler and scammer well known to those who made their living on the strip. A greasy tub with gold-plated aviators and a bad combover, he'd mentioned to Lucy he needed a couple associates for a card counting job he was planning. She passed along the tip to Cera with a warning.

"Shady J's the kind of guy I always make pay upfront," she'd said. "I know you think you're hot shit, but after what happened last time, I hope you learned to watch yourself a little better."

Cera had rolled her eyes. Where did Lucy get off lecturing her about *"last time?"* Sure, she'd accidentally stumbled into the middle of some kind of feud between a pair of gangsters and some other mysterious operator named Vinny, and yes, the two gangsters had nearly killed her right there in Lucy's living room, but that was one time! Whatever happened to the 'three strikes' policy?

Then again, a strange new thought occurred to her, *with what happened today, maybe she was right...?*

Cera dialed Lucy's cell phone. It rang through to voicemail. She called again. Same thing. She re-dialed the number. It went to voicemail again. She dialed the number a fourth time, then a fifth.

Lucy finally answered: "Goddamn, bitch! Have you ever considered that, if someone don't answer their fucking phone, it's 'cause *they don't want to fucking talk to you?*"

"Great to hear from you too, Lucy," Cera said. "How are you, how's your mother?"

"Save it, Cera. Save your bullshit. Recycle it, for all I care. Do something good for once."

"The hell are you talking about?"

"You know goddamn good and well what I'm talking about. You *screwed* me. You fucking screwed me, Cera."

Cera bit her tongue, mustering all her willpower to resist the temptation to ask: "*Isn't that your job?*"

Instead, she adopted a nonchalant tone. "Is this about the 'gangsters in your living room' thing? Look…"

Another phone call came in while she was talking. Cera looked at the screen. It was her internship. She ignored it.

"It's about the goddamn *money*," Lucy snapped. "Yeah, I figured it out. I can't believe that I saved your fucking ass, and then you *still* lied to my face like that."

Cera blinked. "The money?"

"The fucking money, Cera! The cash those two goons had on them. You said we could split it 60-40, and you'd give me the bigger share. And then you fucking switched the cuts on me!"

"Lucy, girl, come on, that was an *accident*," Cera lied through her teeth. "Obviously! Why would I do that?"

"Because you're a *selfish bitch*, Cera." Lucy said it like it was the most obvious thing in the world. "You think I trust you, like we're still friends?"

"Aren't we?"

"After you fucking lied to my face, for a few hundred measly bucks?" She tsked her tongue. "If that's how you treat your friends, you're not gonna have 'em for very long. And in this town, a girl *needs* friends to survive."

"Look," Cera sighed, "you want the truth?"

"You know how to tell the truth?"

"Very funny. Listen — the truth is, I'm in trouble"

"And you think I care? I told you, next time you're in deep shit, don't come calling me."

"Please, Lucy, please," Cera said, genuine desperation leaking into her voice. "It's Shady J. That card counting job? He sold everybody out. I barely managed to make it out before the pit boss broke my neck."

"I told you to be careful with him," Lucy said. "I warned you. But you didn't fucking listen to me, did you?"

"I *did* listen to you! I even got a down payment!" Cera struggled to keep her voice down. "The whole reason I *took* the job was because it came through you. So, the way I see it, part of the responsibility for my current predicament falls on you."

On the other end, Lucy remained silent. Maybe she really did feel some measure of guilt for passing along Shady J's offer.

That was Cera's cue to exploit this newfound advantage to the hilt.

"You ever hear the saying that once you save someone's life, you're responsible for them? Well, truth is, when you came home that night I'd pissed off those two goons… you saved my life." She paused for dramatic effect. "I need you, Lucy. I need your help." Now she adopted a subtle warble in her voice. "As a friend — as maybe my *only* friend — *please*."

Lucy sighed. "What am I supposed to do? I can't go back in time and make Shady J unscrew you."

That was it. Cera had her.

"Well… Shady J *loooves* you, doesn't he?"

"If that's what you want to call it."

"I just need to know where he is. Call him up, talk dirty to him, y'know, get him all riled up, 'till he caves and tells you where to meet him."

"And what then, Cera? Let's say I help you. What are you gonna do? Break his kneecaps? Choke him out? You're a hundred pounds soaking wet, for christ's sake."

"I, uh…" Cera trailed off. "I hadn't quite gotten that far…"

"See, this is your problem, Cera. You never think things through. You want to send Shady J a message that you're not someone to be fucked with, but you *are*. It don't matter how good you are at picking pockets. At the end of the day, you're a small fish in a big pond, and it's filled with fucking sharks. If you were smart, you'd still be doing that internship."

Cera rolled her eyes. "Oh please, don't give me that. Didn't *you* decide you weren't cut out for that straight-world life?"

"Yeah, and I was failing all the classes for our major. You got straight fuckin' A's. And now what, you're just going to throw it all away?"

"Throw *what* away? Waking up every day for the morning commute, wearing some ugly-ass pantsuit, manipulating numbers to help some rich fucks get even richer? No thanks — I got a taste, and it tastes like shit."

"What's the alternative? *This*? 'Cause your life of crime is going *so* splendidly so far."

"Just let *me* worry about me, okay?" Cera sighed. "Bottom line is, I really need your help right now, and I don't got no one else to ask. I'll even pay you back the money I stiffed you, okay?"

"So you admit you stiffed me!"

"Goddamnit Lucy, c'mon!"

Cera held her breath until she replied. "Fine," Lucy groaned. "But it's gonna take more than just the couple hundred bucks you *already* owed me. How much did you get from Shady J?"

Shit.

"…Half upfront," Cera grumbled.

"Good," Lucy said. Cera could practically hear her shit-eating grin through the phone. "I want it all. First, final, and only offer."

Lucy knew exactly how much taking that offer would pain Cera.

"Fine," Cera hissed through gritted teeth. "Deal."

* * *

According to Lucy's intel, Shady J was hiding in a dumpy motel off the 95 outside the city, half an hour out into the desert. Room seven, first floor. First stop, though, was Lucy's new address, to fork over the money.

"How are you even going to get out there?" Lucy asked, slipping the cash into her purse.

"I keep telling you," Cera said. "Let *me* worry about me."

She hung around the nearest parking garage until a distracted tourist with an open purse waddled by, car keys plainly visible. An infant would've taken more notice of their candy being stolen. Cera let herself into what turned out to be a weather-beaten station wagon, turned the key in the ignition, and made for the highway.

Cruising through the sunbaked expanse, Cera pondered her next move.

The goal, she decided, was to acquire the payday she'd been promised. The way she figured it, whoever had paid Shady J to set up the double cross must've given him enough to make it worthwhile — hopefully in cash, and hopefully by the briefcase. All she had to do was get Shady J out of the room, get in, find it, and grab it. A little more complex than lifting a watch off somebody's wrist, but she would figure it out as she went. Call it on-the-job learning.

The first thing she did was scope the place out. There were barely any cars in the lot, meaning most of the rooms were empty. A housekeeper moved slowly from room to room on the second floor, a master keycard dangling from his belt loop. Room seven had the blinds drawn, but shifting lights within suggested an active television, which in turn suggested a viewer. There was somebody home — which meant Lucy's intel was good. Shady J was holed up inside.

The next thing she did was enter the lobby. The girl behind the counter barely looked up from her book, certainly not for long enough to commit Cera's face to memory. Just the way she liked it.

"I have a friend staying in room seven," Cera said. "Could you let him know I'm going to grab us a table at the diner down the road?"

"Sure," mumbled the disinterested girl. "What's your name?"

"It's Lucy," Cera smiled.

She returned to her stolen car. Within minutes, Shady J emerged from the motel room like a baby turtle from its egg, furtively poking his head out of the room and scanning for predators. Cera scrooched down inside her stolen vehicle. His paranoia apparently satisfied, Shady J donned his golden aviators and made a mad dash for his car, where he hoisted himself into the driver's seat and sped away.

Now the clock was ticking. Cera needed to be gone *before* Shady J got back.

She left the car again and climbed the stairs to the second floor. She waited until the housekeeper was between rooms, then casually made her way down the walkway. In the half a second it took to pass him by, she coaxed the keycard from its holster and slipped it into her pocket, just like the pit boss. By the time the housekeeper realized he was locked out of the next room, Cera had already vanished.

The inside of Shady J's room was like any other motel anywhere in the country. An outdated TV, dented mini-fridge, undersized dresser, and deeply stained bed comprised the entirety of the furnishings. Half a pot of cheap coffee sat calcifying on a cold burner. She was hoping to walk in and see a briefcase full of cash on the mattress, but things are never that easy, are they?

Cera began, quickly but methodically, to toss the place. She pulled drawers from the dresser, revealing only a Gideon Bible. She found his suitcase and dumped its contents across the floor: sweat-stained shirts, rumpled slacks, skid-marked undies, unopened toiletries. She removed the back of the toilet tank, hoping to find a submerged baggie. No such luck. Her heart began to beat in double time. Using a dime, she unscrewed the air vent over the toilet and reached into the recesses of the wall. Nothing there either. She used her stolen car keys to rip into the mattress and the pillows. Nothing but fluff.

There was no money, anywhere.

Not a single goddamn cent.

A new thought occurred to her. *What if he got paid with a wire transfer? What then, huh?* Cera kicked Shady J's overturned suitcase in a fit of frustration. *You fucking idiot. Lucy was right. You never fucking think anything through, do you?*

The sound of the doorknob turning interrupted her self-deprecation. She'd taken too long. Shady J was back. Adrenaline rushed through her. She had no way out of the room and nowhere to hide. That only left her with one option.

She grabbed the pot of coffee, wishing it was still hot. Cera reared back with the glass, ready to strike.

As the schlubby backstabber crossed the threshold of the room, he looked up and, for a brief instant, made eye contact with Cera. Behind the lenses of his aviators, his eyes went wide with recognition. Then the coffee pot collided with his jawbone. Glass shattered, and his aviators flew from his face to the floor.

"Jesus fucking Christ!"

Shady J stumbled forward, clutching his face. Cera kicked him in the back of the knee, sending him to the floor. She grabbed one of his shirts from the floor, wrapped it around his neck from behind, and pulled it tight. He bucked and trashed, but Cera held on for dear life, pulling the makeshift noose tighter. Shady J clawed at his throat.

"Where's the money?" Cera barked. "Where's the fucking *money*, you piece of shit?!"

Shady J managed to gasp out three words: "*What—fucking—money?*"

His question hit Cera like a truck. She refused to accept the realization that began to dawn on her. Instead, she pulled the shirt tighter.

"Don't play stupid with me!" she hollered. "Somebody paid you to set everyone up! And I! Want! The! Fucking! Money!"

Shady J gagged, eyes bulging and face burning red. He tried to answer but couldn't form the words. Cera released the tension just enough to let him speak.

"There is… *no*… money…!" Shady J wheezed.

"There's no way you put together a team and then burned us just for shits and fucking giggles!"

"I can't make… your imaginary money… suddenly appear…."

His face had gone from red to blue. His eyes looked like two over-filled balloons, ready to pop. "I'm not... a fucking... magician..."

Cera finally released his throat. He fell forward, sucking down greedy breaths. She dropped the shirt to the floor, her hands shaking.

"Start talking," Cera said.

"You crazy fucking bitch... I had a bad streak, okay?" Shady J massaged his throat. "Got way, way too deep in the red. That can be fatal in my line of work."

"So you put together a card counting job to cover the debt? And then you just *happened* to take a piss *right before* everyone got pinched? *Bullshit.*"

She eyed him warily, expecting him to pounce at any moment. Instead, his only motion was to roll over onto his ass. He sat there, shoulders hunched and eyes downcast — the body language of a man defeated.

"It wasn't my goddamn idea, alright? I wanted no part of it, but wasn't like they left me much choice."

Her eyes narrowed. "Who's 'they'?"

Shady J rolled his eyes. "Don't you know how anything works? *The casino.*"

Cera blinked several times in quick succession. "The casino?" Puzzle pieces started clicking into place inside her brain.

It was an inside job the whole fucking time.

She took an involuntary step backwards, catching herself on the bedframe.

How did I miss that?

"They came to me, said I had two choices. One, they could, uh, 'settle my account,' *permanently.* Or two, I pull together a team of suckers for them to bust." He shrugged. "I chose option two, on account of how I like being alive."

"But... why? How is a phony card counting bust worth that much to them?"

"Two words, kid." He counted them on his fingers, chuckling cruelly. "Annual. Reviews. Everybody's got a boss breathing down their neck, demanding results. A big bust before reviews means happy managers, happy investors, and a nice big bonus come holiday time."

Cera sank onto the bed, mirroring his defeated posture.

All this goddamn trouble for some jackoff's fucking Christmas bonus. How fucking... boring.

Of course that's what it came down to. Why should it come down to anything else? That's all anything was about — whose pockets were getting lined, and who was getting screwed over to line them. It was just business and bloodsuckers all the way down, no matter where you go. All the anger that had propelled her to this point broke, leaving behind only a quiet, resentful disgust.

"Yep," Shady J kept on chuckling. "Win-win. Everyone walks away happy — except the folks like us, of course." He winked.

"Like *us*?" Cera snapped. "Don't lump me in with you. We are *nothing* alike."

Shady J laughed harder. "Aren't we? Couple a two-bit cons, not a goddamn dollar to their name, burned every bridge with anyone stupid enough to ever call them a friend. And now you're here: today's big loser," He smiled wide, revealing long, nicotine-yellowed teeth. "Am I wrong?"

Cera swallowed hard. "Fuck you," she spat.

Shady J evidently found this response hilarious. "If you want to, then sure, baby, I'm game," he replied with a lecherous grin.

Cera nearly recoiled in disgust, but an idea occurred to her. Instead, she adopted a soft, sensual expression. "It *has* been a long day," she purred. "Maybe it would help relieve the stress..."

Shady J's eyebrows shot up to the top of his head. "Really?" He cleared his throat. "I mean, of course, baby." He grabbed his aviators from the floor and resettled them overtop his eyes. "Let daddy help you relax..."

Cera came closer and offered her hand to help him up from the floor. When he grabbed it, she yanked him off balance and drove her knee into his crotch. As he crumpled back down, her hand made a quick detour into his pocket. She swiped his keys and replaced them with the keys to the stolen sedan in the parking lot. Smiling, she leaned down and whispered in his ear: "Lucy says you're a two-pump chump, by the way."

She took his golden sunglasses and left him groaning on the motel floor.

• • •

Piloting Shady J's car back through the darkening desert toward the eternally illuminated city, the inescapable reek of failure enveloped her.

She left the truck outside the same parking garage where she stole the sedan, then walked the mile and a half back to the dumpy motel room of her own. By the time she got there, she'd made up her mind. With a crushing sense of resignation, she would return to her internship, get her boring-ass degree, wake up each day for the morning commute, marry some schmuck, shit out a couple kids, and die of preventable disease in middle age.

What else was there to do?

Outside her door, she checked her phone. There was a new voicemail, from her supervisor at the firm. Due to her repeated absences, they'd canceled her internship. So much for that. *Do not pass go. Do not collect $200.* Cera sighed. *Maybe if I grovel enough, they'll let me come back…*

Exhaustion ached within every bone in her body. Wanting nothing more than to slip into a dreamless sleep, she opened the door to her room. Her heart caught in her throat. A stranger waited inside, calmly reading a well-worn copy of *The Myth of Sisyphus* by lamplight.

He was only a head taller than her, but broad and well-built, like a linebacker. Despite the desert heat, he wore a black leather jacket, matching leather gloves, and designer jeans. A pearl dangled from a silver chain hanging from one ear. His face was round, red and puffy, with a deep checkmark-shaped scar in his right cheek, as if a chunk of flesh had been dug out with a knife. The stranger put his book on the table, smiling as if he'd been expected.

"Don't freak out," he said.

Cera didn't, but neither did she respond, instead lingering in the doorway and considering bolting.

"Don't run, either. I just want to talk."

"Who the fuck are you?"

"Honestly? Big fan of your work. Not here to hurt you." He held up three fingers. "Scout's honor."

Cera stepped inside the room, steeling herself — prepared to run, or fight, at the first sign of movement. Her eyes darted around the room, considering options. The stranger watched her eyes as they moved around the space. They lingered on the mini fridge, then resettled on the intruder.

"I understand you met a couple of my competitors a few nights ago," the stranger said.

"Again," Cera growled, "who the fuck *are* you? And why are you here?"

"You haven't figured it out?" The man chuckled. "The name's Vinny."

Vinny? Vinny… Why did that name sound so familiar?

"My competitors you met, they're in the hospital now. Apparently, Elmore has a new hole in the side of his neck." Vinny let out a low, appreciative whistle. "Impressive."

Elmore. That had been one of the gangsters at Lucy's old place.

Wait a second. Vinny. I remember now…

"So that means," Cera turned the pieces over in her mind. "*You're* the guy who was double-crossing the two fucks who tried to kill me."

"Which you only know," Vinny nodded, "because you picked the wrong pocket. One of my guys."

Cera took a beat. He didn't seem upset — merely stating a fact. She made an unusual decision at that moment. She decided to tell the truth. After all she'd been through today, why not?

"Yeah, I picked his pocket. Okay? It's what I do. So fucking what?

A girl's gotta eat, and I ain't got nobody putting food on my plate but me. If he had such sensitive information on his phone, maybe he shouldn't've been stumbling around blind drunk at fucking ten in the morning."

"Let me ask you a question." Vinny didn't wait for her to agree. "How long have you been doing this?"

Whatever inquiry she might've been expecting, it wasn't that. "What do you mean?"

"Getting by like this. Y'know, picking pockets, stabbing dudes in the neck, that sort of thing."

Technically, it had been *Lucy* who'd done the stabbing, with the heel of one of her stilettos, but Cera didn't see any reason Vinny needed to know that. Maybe she could even use that to her advantage.

"Since I was sixteen. And you know what? I'm good at it."

She casually reached down and opened the fridge. Vinny let her go, still tracking her motions with his eyes.

"I've always done what I needed to do to survive," she continued. "Isn't that what everyone does? So what the fuck do you want, huh? Payback? Revenge?"

Cera grabbed one of the beers and, without wasting any motion, smashed it open over the fridge. She brandished the broken bottle and let her fury flare.

"OR MAYBE YOU WANT A HOLE IN YOUR NECK TO MATCH?!"

Her words echoed around the mildew-stained room. Vinny let them hang in the air without reacting. Then he began to clap, slowly at first, but then faster and more vigorously. He slapped his palms together like a satisfied audience member at a casino stage show.

"Fan-fucking-tastic," Vinny said, smiling from ear to ear. "That is *exactly* what I was hoping you'd say."

"That…" Her hands shook from the rush of adrenaline. "*What*?"

"Think you're misunderstanding why I'm here," Vinny answered. "You see, I'm something of a… cultivator of promising talent, you could say. It's how I give back to the community. So when I hear about, say, how one of my rivals got taken out by a new, talented young operator, why, that's the kind of thing I have to see for myself."

She still held the bottle like a switchblade, suspicious. "Get to the point."

"The point…" Vinny paused, running his gloved hand through his black, oily hair. "…is I'd like to offer you a position in my organization."

Cera titled her head, letting the bottle fall to her side. *Was this whole thing just… an interview?*

"What, like a job?"

"Well," Vinny scratched his scar, "think of it more like… an internship. *Paid*, of course."

She smiled. It took her half a heartbeat to consider. Didn't Lucy say she needed friends if she was gonna survive in this town?

Fuck groveling for some straight-world job I don't even want. Fuck working for tightwads in overpriced suits. Fuck being some asshole's Christmas bonus.

Two words — Fuck. It.

This was where she felt alive.

"Well, Vinny, that depends on one thing…"

Vinny grinned, knowing exactly what was coming. Cera put on her best negotiating face, ready to reject his first offer, no matter how much it was.

"How *much* does it pay?"

...AND SATAN CAME WITH THEM

I think a great deal about the Book of Job," announced Father McCullers.

The priest stood before a workbench in the corner of a rotting shed, eyeing a selection of rusty implements. Pliers. Hacksaw. Screwdrivers. He ran his hand from item to item, as if searching for the proper tool for an unknown job. A smile split his face like a wound.

"Compared to the Gospel of Matthew, for instance, but, of course, that's the New Testament..."

Drill. Nail gun. Arbor press.

"But even compared to Psalms, Isaiah, or Exodus…"

Angle grinder. Soldering iron.

"Job — the Book, that is, not the man — teaches us values not explored so fully elsewhere in the Scripture…"

Hammers. Bleach. Assorted cleaners.

"Ask yourself. Where were we, pitiful creatures, when He laid the foundations of the E arth?" He chuckled to himself. "Where were *you?*"

More exotic fare: Syringes, dripping clear solutions of sinister intent. Little silver silos of liquid nitrogen. Piano wire.

"You see, my point is, I suppose…" He turned around, sharp white teeth gleaming in the dark. "I fear Job's lessons are *undervalued*."

The Father turned. Before him, Allen Myers—a dairy farmer by trade, blessed in the worldly riches of land, beasts, and children—lay strapped to a table of darkly-stained oak. Sweat beaded across his broad forehead. Tears leaked from bloodshot blue eyes. Tightly fastened leather straps bound his wrists to the table, rendering his fingertips the blueish white of bloodless flesh. Saliva burbled around the ball gag between his teeth.

"Gahd, Gahd," he sobbed. "Wha' have I done to deserve thif?"

"Shhh, shhh." Father McCullers ran the bony spindles of his fingers across his face, gently wiping away his tears. "The wages of sin are *death*, my child." He rested his thumb against his right eye and pressed, feeling the vitreous mass depress as Myers screamed against his gag. The priest licked his lips as he drove deeper, savoring the gel-filled orb warping around his thumb, then released his eye and returned to the workbench. "But perhaps you deserve a more proper explanation. You're a man of faith, are you not? God-fearing? Rich in the blessings of the Lord?"

Myers nodded vigorously, as if he might escape captivity on the virtue of his good works alone.

"Of course you are, my child. You're a good man. But is it for nothing that you are God-fearing? After all, the faith of 'good' men is a shallow faith indeed. Where is your faith in the face of pain? In the face of loss? When have you anointed yourself in ash in the depths of your sorrow, all your blessings reduced to dust, still faithful to He who takes away?"

Myers howled like a wounded animal.

"You see, this is exactly my point about Job. Even ignoring the theodicean elements, it raises so many questions," Father McCullers continued leisurely, as if this were any other sermon. "And I quote, 'there was a day when the sons of God came to present themselves before the Lord, and Satan came with them.' And Satan came with

them? Strange, isn't it? The Lord received Satan like an old friend —
or a prodigal son! — welcomed back into his Father's home."

He paused to examine each individual line carved into Allen
Myers' contorted face.

"You see, we forget all too often the *breadth* of His creations. The
day, *and* the night. The dove, *and* the Leviathan. Good…" He picked
up a pair of pliers, appraising it by the crimson light of the fire burning in its corner hearth. "And Evil."

He turned, eyes invisible in the shifting shadows cast by the
fire, save his irises gleaming like a cat's in the night. A wet, sobbing
scream rolled up Myers' throat, muffled by the gag.

"Behold." The Father smiled, leaning in with the pliers. "You are
vile. I will lay my hand upon thy mouth."

Myers thrashed against his restraints.

* * *

Earlier that morning, Elizabeth Wilson, a stooped and grey-headed
woman newly arrived in town, took a seat for the first time in the
backmost pew of St. Andrew the Apostle's, a temple of rust-colored
bricks on Broad Street in Waynesboro. Her hands spasmed, not from
age, but from a cold rush of adrenaline as she waited for the service
to begin.

Fifteen years. Fifteen years since Malcolm had been stolen from
her. The call to identify the body had been little more than formality.
The mass of mangled meat no longer resembled her Malcolm. At
nights, visions of her husband's ruined body haunted her, just as he'd
appeared when the police pulled the sheet away: fleshless, seeping,
the details of the face burned away, the familiar curves of his nose
and cheeks erased, replaced by a mask of charred, blistered muscle
clinging to the skull. She'd vomited on the morgue floor.

After the initial shock, Elizabeth had attempted to adjust to a wid-
ow's life. Her mother had done it before her; now was her turn to
bear the cross. Between the despair, the fatigue, and all the practical

matters that needed attending, she barely even noticed that Father Henry McCullers, a humble homilist who'd joined the congregation not five years before, transferred to another church less than two weeks after her husband's death. Years passed. Her life approached something resembling a new normalcy.

Then, five years after Malcom's passing, a man in Fulton County was found mutilated almost beyond recognition. He'd been found in a shed of unknown construction or ownership, deep in the woods. Howard Bigler, 45, lumber yard owner, family man, devoted attendee at St. Stephen's in McConnellsburg. Then, four years after that, in Westmoreland County, Daniel Shindledecker, 62, CPA, father of four, grandfather of eight, and faithful parishioner at Our Lady of Grace in Greensburg, discovered in an abandoned mill off a closed road in an empty corner of the county. Elizabeth felt a profound disquiet, a still small voice whispering in her ear.

When Bigler had been discovered, she wondered if he'd been mutilated by the same hand that had tortured her husband, but she forced the thought into the depths of her mind, where it festered like an abscess in her soul. But upon Shindledecker's discovery, wonder blossomed into conviction, peace devolved into obsession, and thought demanded to become deed.

In researching these killings, Elizabeth discovered something that stoked the flames smoldering in her breast. At each of the victim's churches, Father Henry McCullers had invariably arrived a few years before the murder, and left shortly thereafter — just as he had come and gone from the church where she and Malcolm had been wed, now defiled by a darkness no light could ever illuminate.

By the time she made this discovery and tracked down the priest's whereabouts, he had already haunted St. Andrew the Apostle's for three years, more than enough time to have picked out a new victim. Evil followed McCullers like a shadow, and the time had come for Elizabeth to give life for life, eye for eye, tooth for tooth, hand for hand, foot for foot, burning for burning, wound for wound, and stripe for stripe, so sayeth the Lord.

The familiar drawl of Father McCuller's voice ripped Elizabeth away from her thoughts as he took the podium to deliver the morning's homily. The sight of him — gaunt and hollow-cheeked, with eyes like two small coals burning in their sockets — provoked the taste of bile in her throat.

"One day," McCullers declared, "there was a man, blameless and upright, who feared God and avoided evil. And on that day, the sons of God came to present themselves before the Lord." He paused, savoring the next line. "…And Satan came with them."

Elizabeth recognized the sermon opening. It was the same one Father McCullers had delivered the morning before he butchered her husband.

"And the Lord asked Satan, 'where do you come from?' And Satan answered the Lord, 'from roaming the earth, patrolling it' — as a master might patrol his fields, overseeing the work of his servants."

Father McCullers paused to cast his gaze upon the crowd. Elizabeth looked away as the spotlight of his eyes passed over her pew.

"What an answer Satan dares to give the Lord! To suggest that while He controls the Heavens, the Adversary stalks His creations, sowing seeds of doubt and chaos in the hearts of men. And yet the Lord does not rebuke him, but instead *engages* him, asking if Satan has seen this blameless and upright man, most loyal of all His servants." The Father drummed his fingers against the pulpit, a twitch playing at the corners of his mouth. "And sharp-tongued Satan dares again to question the Lord, to declare that this man is only loyal for God has blessed him! Were God to revoke these blessings, surely this man would blaspheme Him to His face!"

Elizabeth closed her eyes and took deep, shuddering breaths. She reached a hand into her red leather purse and wrapped her fingers around the handle of her recently purchased Smith & Wesson .38 Special. No. Not yet. Not here.

"And, amazingly, again God does not rebuke him!" The priest slammed his hand against the podium. "No, instead, the Lord offers this man's life up to Satan's control. This man, upright and blameless, is delivered into Satan's hand by none other than the Lord himself. Why? Why! Why, I ask you!"

Sweat shone on the priest's forehead, his breathing ragged with passion.

"But who are *we* to question the machinations of He who laid the foundations of the Earth?! He who shut the sea behind doors, who has shown the dawn its place so it might shake the wicked from the earth!"

Father McCullers paused, his voice still reverberating through the high-ceilinged hall. He scanned the room with his two burning coals, and they came to rest on Elizabeth.

"For what are we, what is our suffering, before His majesty, His knowledge, His infinite wisdom? Indeed, if the Lord sees fit to deliver us into Satan's hand, it is for reasons that are not ours to question." He smiled, and she raised her hand to her mouth, fighting back the vomit. "For the *fear* of the Lord is *wisdom*, and avoiding evil is *understanding*."

Elizabeth rose, stumbled to the doors, ran to the restroom, and released the contents of her stomach into nearest porcelain bowl. She lay against the cool tile of the bathroom floor until she could no longer hear Father McCullers' voice booming from the pulpit. The homily ended, she returned quietly to her pew and waited, her knee bouncing anxiously, until the time came for confession. She stood in line outside the ornate wooden coffin, silently mouthing familiar prayers for guidance. She clutched her purse to her chest as she crossed the threshold into the confessional and the door shut behind her. The outline of Father McCullers' face shifted behind the black lace of the confessional screen.

"Bless me Father," Elizabeth whispered, her voice shaking, "for I have sinned. It has been more than a year since my last confession."

"Speak, my child." The Father turned behind the screen. The lights of his eyes flashed in the darkness.

"I have carried hatred in my heart," Elizabeth said. Tears welled in the corners of her tired eyes and ran through the ravines carved into her wrinkled face. "For years, like a garden, I have tended to it, fed it, let it grow wild in my soul."

"Refrain from anger," the priest answered. "And turn from wrath; it leads only to evil."

"I have *already* let myself be led to evil," Elizabeth responded, her voice raw. She gripped the rosary beads around her neck that had once belonged to her husband. "I have desired vengeance, planned it, longed for it. Plotted foul deeds against one who has wronged me."

"Did you lay the foundations of the Earth?" Father McCullers said.

Elizabeth didn't answer, still thumbing her rosary beads.

"No? Then vengeance does not belong to you. It is not for us to weigh the scales of justice. Vengeance belongs to the Lord. Trust in Him, for He tells us that the wicked will know He is the Lord thy God when He lays His vengeance upon them."

"Is it not possible," Elizabeth asked, removing her hand from the beads, "that mortal creatures, like you or I, might be the tools He uses to enact that vengeance?"

He laughed hollowly. "Who do you seek vengeance against, my child?"

Elizabeth slipped her hand into her purse. "A man who has wronged me, who has spilled innocent blood. A man who claims to be of the Lord, but acts in service of the Adversary."

Again she gripped the handle of her pistol, her hand trembling inside her bag.

"The scripture tells us no blood is innocent, child. *All* have sinned and fallen short of the glory of God," the Father replied, his eyes burning holes through the screen between them. "Seek you vengeance, so that through your sinning grace may increase? Shall you accept only good from God, and not evil? Is it your place to return what God has seen fit to deliver you?"

The Father placed his hand against the screen and leaned in close, whispering like a nighttime breeze through desolate treetops.

"For perhaps you were delivered to the hands of this man who wronged you as Job was delivered unto Satan — by the Lord himself." The white teeth of his smile shone behind the screen. "The faith of good men means nothing. The faith of the suffering means everything. Now, will you anoint yourself in ash, or will you curse God and die?"

Elizabeth didn't answer, her hand still wrapped around the gun.

"You will be forgiven for your sins of wrath. Say three Our Fathers so that you may grow in the virtue of temperance, and make an Act of Contrition."

Elizabeth took a shuddering breath, and released the gun. She repeated to herself the same message as before: Not yet. Not here.

"O my God, I am heartily sorry for having offended Thee," Elizabeth repeated, choking on her tears, "and I detest all my sins, because I dread the loss of heaven, and the pains of hell; but most of all because they offend Thee, my God, Who are good and deserving of all my love. I firmly resolve, with the help of Thy grace, to sin no more and avoid the near occasions of sin. Amen."

"Amen," Father McCullers repeated, retreating back into the shadows of the confessional. "Now go in peace."

• • •

That evening, Allen Myers howled in misery, now eyeless and blind as Samson, as Father McCullers clamped his pliers around the soft and supple tongue. One of Myers arms was now free from his restraints, but it merely hung limply from the table, the bones pressed into dozens of useless fragments. Blood dripped from his fingertips where the nails had once been. A severed foot lay on the floor in a circle of bloody wire, the stump cauterized by liquid nitrogen, though crimson still dripped slowly through the blue-white charring.

The Father could feel the tissue beginning to tear as the fleshy cable that anchored the tongue to the bottom of the mouth protested against the pressure. Blood leaked from Myers' toothless mouth down his chin. The cable snapped and the tongue became untied, the rudder ripping free of the ship. The priest regarded the twitching pink and purple muscle between the pliers as Myers bellowed in inarticulable anguish, reduced to a quivering mass of suffering.

"Don't worry, my child," Father McCullers smiled, letting his tongue drop from the pliers to the dirt. "I've done you a great favor. The scripture tells us that tongue is a world of evil that corrupts the whole body. And so I've removed it for you!" He laughed, caressing his victim's face with the tenderness of a lover. "And how your eyes caused you to sin! So I have plucked them for you!"

Myers shook his head back and forth, praying for the Lord to deliver him from this evil, praying for justice, but most of all, praying for death. His lips moved slowly in a pantomime of speech as he pleaded with a silent God.

Seeing this, Father McCullers chortled with glee.

"Praying, even now? Truly, what a blameless and upright man you are." He patted the side of his disfigured face, tsking his tongue.

So intently focused on his contorted and screeching victim was Father McCullers that he failed to hear tires rolling to a stop on the dirt outside.

From her car, which she had been driving lightless, painstakingly following the priest's tire tracks by the light of the moon, Elizabeth emerged and stood, upright and full of blame, holding the revolver tight in her bony fist. From the shack, she heard Myers weeping and shrieking, his voice stripped of its dignity and humanity. She wondered if Malcolm had sounded the same.

She crept toward the door, blood pounding in her ears, and slowly pushed it open. Father McCullers hovered over his victim, gripping Myers' face in his hand, and staring intently into the twin voids where his eyes had once been.

"Shhh. Shhh. All of this can be over. Will you anoint yourself with ash? Or will you curse God and die?"

The man slowly nodded, blood gurgling from his mouth.

Elizabeth raised the pistol, aiming through the shadow at the black-robed figure illuminated by the shifting flames.

"Yes, that's what you want? You renounce Christ and all his works? You will curse God and die?"

Elizabeth squeezed the trigger.

Her gun spoke as if out of a whirlwind.

The bullet entered between Father McCullers' ribs and exited out the other side, bringing with it a spray of blood that sizzled on the fire. He slipped from atop the table to the ground clutching his wound. He turned to Elizabeth, recognition shining in his eyes.

"You?"

She fired again, spinning him round as the bullet caught his shoulder. Again, shattering his kneecap. Again, burying the metal slug deep in his gut. He lay on the ground, gasping for life as he watched Elizabeth above him.

"Still you have not learned your lesson!" The Father laughed, sending plumes of blood arcing from his mouth. "This is not your judgment to make! Where were you when He stilled the sea's proud waves? When the morning stars sang in chorus and all the sons of God shouted for joy?" He coughed a scarlet mass onto the front of his robes. "Where were you when He laid the foundations of the Earth?"

Elizabeth stepped forward and pushed the barrel of the gun between his teeth.

"Where were *you*?"

She pulled the trigger.

The Father slumped to the dirt, the back of his head seeping into the earth. A single bullet still rested in the chamber. From the table, Myers trashed, his prayers answered, an angel of death delivered unto him.

But as Elizabeth appraised him, she found him broken beyond repair and past the point of saving, much like herself. But, unlike her, he would die on his own within the hour, and though he'd wished for death intensely this single evening, she had waited for its embrace for fifteen years. Fifteen excruciating years, and she could bear the waiting no longer.

"It is finished."

She turned away, bowed her head, and placed the barrel to her temple.

"O my God, I am heartily sorry for having offended Thee," Elizabeth whispered, filled by an emptiness deeper than the sources of the sea.

"I detest all my sins, because I dread the loss of heaven, and the pains of hell; but most of all because they offend Thee, my God, Who are good and deserving of all my love."

She could no longer hear Myers' cries, could feel nothing but the metal pressed against her head.

"I firmly resolve, with the help of Thy grace, to sin no more and avoid the near occasions of sin."

She was neither frightened nor dismayed. God would be with her, no matter where she went.

"Amen."

She pulled the trigger, and went in peace.

TWENTY COLUMN INCHES

Raymond Reynolds, a disheveled and rather loosely put together fellow wearing a Stetson of timeworn black felt, panicked as the door behind him creaked open. He plucked the smoking joint stuffed with sticky sativa from his lips, smooshed it into the ashtray beside the back door of the Detweiler County municipal building, and hoped his eyes weren't overly bloodshot. Luckily, his new companion was not a cop or a county commissioner, but an older woman with an elaborately coiffed mahogany mane in an oversized trench coat and impenetrable sunglasses. Ray breathed a sigh of relief, but then cursed himself for wasting weed. That was some good shit he just smashed into the pile of butts and ash.

The woman, standing beside him and watching the rain pour down on the municipal lot, produced a pack of cigarettes from insider her coat. She extended the pack toward Ray, who shook his head.

"No thanks. Don't smoke."

She cocked an eyebrow and looked at the hand-rolled wrapping Ray had just extinguished in the ashtray, but merely shrugged and brought a cigarette to her red-painted lips. Ray turned his collar up and pulled his hat down, preparing to venture forth into the rain. He had to get back to the newsroom to write up the county commissioners meeting. His editor wanted twenty column inches, which Ray had tried to warn against. Nothing interesting ever happened with the commissioners.

"Reynolds, right?" Ray turned to look at her. "We should talk."

"Should we?"

"I have a story for you." Her voice creaked like a rusted hinge.

"Well, greetings before business, as my dad used to say." Ray extended his hand. "Raymond Reynolds, crime reporter, Haroldston Herald." The woman grimaced, sucking down cigarette smoke. He frowned and retracted his hand. "You see, how greetings usually go, is one person introduces themselves, then the other person goes, you see…"

"But I'm not important."

"Oh? Well, we got that in common."

The woman let out something halfway between a scoff and a chuckle. "Aren't you clever." She smirked in a peculiar way, the right half of her mouth curling upwards while the left remained inert.

"Not that I don't appreciate it," Ray said, "but flattery won't convince me to write whatever it is you got for me."

"What would?"

Ray shrugged. "Dropping this silly lil' act couldn't hurt?"

Her eyebrows rose above the rims of her sunglasses. "Couldn't hurt *you*, maybe."

"Uh-huh. Look." He folded his arms. "Even off the record, I don't take tips from people won't tell me their name."

"I could be… an *anonymous* source."

"Yeah, that ain't how that works. You want to talk, you put your name to it. And *then*, if you ask nice, I won't put it in print."

A long moment slipped past as rain drip-dropped against the asphalt. Just as Ray was prepared to walk away, the woman sighed. "Abigail." Ray made little circles with his hand, as if reeling in a fishing line. "Connors."

"Uh-*huh*. Abigail Connors," extending his hand again, "pleased to make your acquaintance." The woman took his hand limply in her own.

"Charmed," she said.

"So what's the story, morning glory?"

She exhaled sharply from her nose, sending twin plumes of acrid smoke wafting toward him. "You know Allen Harbaugh, of course."

Ray nodded. He was the chair of the Detweiler County commissioners, a squat and balding man with a monotone drawl who seemed determined to make each meeting of the board as dreadfully dull as possible. "Do you know," she asked, "what he did before his retirement, and subsequent election?"

"Construction."

"Founder of Harbaugh Construction, as a matter of fact, who just so happen to have been awarded every lucrative county contract since his election..."

Ray adjusted his hat. "Yeah, we looked into that a while back. He stepped down from the position before he even ran for office. Even talked off the record to a lawyer. Said it shouldn't be an issue, so long as he had removed himself from his business interests."

"You think these contracts are coincidence?"

He shrugged. "I mean, if they bid the lowest, they bid the lowest, y'know?"

She shook her head. "I'd expect better from the fourth estate." She flicked the butt to the ground and walked past him, turning her collar against the rain. "Follow the money, Reynolds."

After she turned the corner, Ray plucked his joint from the ashtray, brushed off a dusting of ash, and reignited it. The smoke, previously tinged with a floral sweetness, tasted now of tar.

• • •

The next afternoon, Ray sat in the driver's seat of his battered Bronco puffing on a joint in the parking lot outside the municipal building, slowly filling the cabin with sticky-sweet smoke as he watched rain-swollen clouds roll eastward across the Pennsylvania sky. In one of his jean pockets was a folded sheet of paper, detailing his Right-to-Know request for any and all documents related to the county's contracts with Harbaugh Construction. In the other was a small baggie containing a single nugget of weed, picked up earlier that afternoon from his roommate, weed dealer, and best friend Johnny.

"One whole marijuana," Johnny had remarked, incredulous. "Don't smoke it all in one place."

"It ain't for me. It's for work." Ray had tried to give him ten bucks.

"For work?" Johnny had waved his hand away. "Have the newspaper send me an invoice."

"I'm sure my editor will *love* that…"

Now waiting for his man outside the municipal building, Ray gazed intently at his phone. He'd been digging through the Harbaugh Construction website for nearly twenty minutes, not quite sure what he was looking for, if anything.

Wait. There.

He paused to look at a photo that caught his eye. It had been posted on the company's thirty-year anniversary, and showed Allen Harbaugh and his staff posing with rigid smiles on their first day at work decades earlier. Beside Harbaugh, clinging to his arm like tinsel to a Christmas tree, was the woman who had approached him with the tip about Harbaugh. She wore a proud smile, both sides of her mouth turned upward.

"Hey there, Abigail…"

Funny thing was, there were no Connors in the area, at least not that Ray knew. He didn't know everyone exactly, but kept tabs on who had beef with whom, tracking generations-long familial disputes that spilled over into his beat with some regularity. If there was a feud between the Harbaughs and another family, like these alleged Connors, Ray wagered he'd already have known about it.

A sharp rapping at his window interrupted his musings. Ray choked on a lungful of hot smoke. Looking over, he saw a thin-lipped and prematurely gray-headed figure in a cheap suit: David

Wells, county administrator, a beleaguered bureaucrat who spent his days shuffling paperwork for the commissioners. Ray unlocked his Bronco doors.

"Christ, Reynolds, have a little courtesy, huh?" Wells said, waving his hand in an ill-fated attempt to dissipate the cloud of pungent smoke that filled the truck. "I gotta go back in the office."

Ray was too preoccupied with regurgitating his lungs to respond. He pulled the bag of weed from his pocket and tossed it in Wells' lap. Wells appraised the marijuana nugget like Indy beholding the Holy Grail.

"How much?" Wells asked.

Ray thought about it. "Twenty bucks," he gasped between coughs.

The bureaucrat fished out a twenty and placed it into Ray's cup holder. He moved to exit the truck, but Ray held up a finger.

"What? The longer I sit here, the more I smell like getting fired."

"I have something else for you," Ray wheezed, "but first..." He showed him the photo on his phone and pointed to the woman. "Do you know her?"

"Harbaugh's ex-wife? Sure. Why?"

Ray finally finished coughing. "No reason," he smiled, teary-eyed. He pulled the papers from his other pocket and passed them to Wells. "These are for you."

Wells took them and read the request over. He rolled his eyes. "What are you after, Ray?"

Ray shrugged.

"You know," Wells said, "I could probably get away with denying this request for being overly broad. *Any and all* documents on Harbaugh contracts? County's been working with them for years."

Ray nodded, tapping his fingers together in front of his mouth. "Funny. That's also 'bout as long as I been sellin' you the best bud in town."

Wells grimaced. "Mmm."

"Come on. Isn't this, like, your job?"

"*Part* of my job. You have any idea how much time this'll take me?"

Ray stuck out his lip in an exaggerated pout. "Would it help if I said pretty please?"

Wells sighed. "Fine. Just give me a bit of time. I'll get you the records. Just don't go sticking my name in anything."

"No worries. Anonymous source."

• • •

Two weeks passed before Wells got Ray what he'd formally requested pursuant to state law, longer than the law technically allotted. Ray could see why it had taken so long. The folder, held together by an oversized rubber band, was thick enough to stop a bullet.

"My magnum opus," Wells said when he handed it over, again sitting in Ray's passenger seat. "Think this can get me a discount off my next order?"

Ray shook his head. "Technically, trading favors is a violation of my professional ethics…"

"And dealing to sources *isn't*?" Ray raised a finger to respond, but paused. The man had a point. Wells pressed on. "I'm not sure what you're looking for in there, but if this has anything to do with Eleanor, I'd watch yourself."

"Eleanor?"

"Harbaugh's ex. The one you'd asked about. She's been trying to stir up trouble for him ever since they split. Sent out mailers during his reelection campaign accusin' him of being a RINO."

"Musta been a messy divorce."

"Left her for another woman," Wells nodded. "Don't see his new wife around much anymore, though."

"Tell you the truth, Eleanor mighta had sumptin to do with my curiosity."

"Careful. Whatever story she said she had for you, it ain't outta the goodness of her heart."

"So? It never is. But that don't mean it ain't true."

He started reading through the folder that night, sitting on the collection of lumps he and Johnny called a couch with joint in hand and a well-worn copy of *At Folsom Prison* spinning on his turntable. There were hundreds of pages of bids, contracts, and records of payments, dating back decades. After several hours of squinting at the undersized font through the smoke and lamplight, a pattern began to emerge.

The county had worked on and off with Harbaugh Construction since the company's founding in 1979. They'd often submitted bids for projects, but were rarely the lowest bidder. But after Harbaugh was elected to the board of county commissioners in 2005, the frequency of contracts skyrocketed. In fact, Ray noticed, they were still only the lowest bidder maybe a third of the time, but received nearly every contract for which they had entered a bid. Things weren't adding up, namely, the dollar signs. In almost every case, the county was paying out somewhere in the neighborhood of fifteen to twenty percent more than what was listed in the bids, contracts, or invoices. According to his napkin math, over $600,000 of taxpayer funds had vanished into the aether over the last fourteen years. Another $400,000 or so could've been saved if the county had contracted out to lower bidders in the first place. Ray wasn't a lawyer, but if it looks like embezzlement and quacks like embezzlement...

He cracked his knuckles, opened his laptop, and got to work. He sent a message to Harbaugh's official county email address requesting an interview on a story he was working on "about questions related to the county's contracts with Harbaugh Construction." Three joints later, he had the bones of the most interesting county commissioner story he'd ever written, at twenty-five column inches.

• • •

Twenty-six joints, four emails, three days, and two voicemails later, Ray still hadn't heard from Harbaugh. He'd already waited long enough. Maybe too long. Eleanor had already earned her own folder in his inbox for her messages inquiring about the story, all signed "Abigail Connors." For all he knew, she had already pulled her femme fatale act with WKKA, the Fox affiliate across the county line, who would probably fall for the schtick. More importantly, his editor would have his guts for garters if they beat him to the story. But there was no way Ray could, in good conscience, go to print without some kind of comment from the man himself. Even an official "no comment" from Harbaugh or, more likely, from his lawyer, would be enough. Time for the nuclear option. His stomach turned at the thought, but, as his dad used to say, half the job was just showing up. One of many lessons Ray the old man had never seemed to listen to himself.

It was a brisk Saturday afternoon lit by cold, pale sunlight when Ray pulled up outside of Harbaugh's Victorian manor on what passed for the ritzy side of Haroldston, the Detweiler County seat, where Clayton Avenue's neatly manicured lawns and water features stood in stark contrast to the entropy that had slowly engulfed the rest of town over the preceding decades. But the pale green paint of Harbaugh's home had grown peeled and faded, the gutters stuffed with dead leaves, and the lawn wildly unkempt, as if he'd given up on maintaining the outward appearance of wealth his neighbors on either side still enjoyed.

Ray had lit a joint on the way over to calm his nerves, which had accomplished the exact opposite. His heart throbbed in his throat at the thought of knocking on the door. Seeking counsel, he called the smartest man he knew.

Johnny answered with a lung-splitting cough.

"Dude," Ray skipped the hello, "what if Harbaugh pulls a gun on me?"

"*What*?" The sound of a bong bubbled in the background.

"That commissioner guy I was telling you about. I'm outside his house."

"All them wild-ass stories you tell me about your rambling days, and you're scared of some pasty bureaucrat?" Johnny audibly exhaled a cloud of smoke. "Didn't you, like, fight off an entire gang of human traffickers with nothing but a box of fireworks?"

Ray rolled his eyes. "It was only two guys, and that ain't exactly how it happened."

"But it was *something* like that?"

"Yeah," Ray shrugged. "Sumpthin' like that."

"So what're you worried about? This guy's a *public servant*, dude. He's not going to shoot you."

"Not a very good one. He might could."

"Then bring that thick-ass folder you've been lugging around with you."

"I don't think it's *actually* bulletproof…"

"Look Ray, let me give you a piece of stoner wisdom that was once passed on to me — if you ever feel like you're being paranoid, you're probably just being paranoid."

Ray considered this. "Seems like good advice."

"It is. Now hurry up — I just got my copy of the final cut and I need you to get out of the newsroom at a decent hour so we can get blitzed and watch it."

"The wha?"

"Blade Runner, dude!" He adopted a strange accent. "*'It's a shame she won't live! But then again, who does?'*"

"We'll see what happens," Ray said. "Thanks, Johnny."

With that, he put away his phone and killed the rest of the joint with a long, deep pull. He emerged from the Bronco wreathed in smoke, flicked the roach to the street, approached the withering home, and rang the bell.

The door opened. Harbaugh, one of the few people Ray knew shorter than him, peered up at him through the crack in the doorway.

"Reynolds," he said simply, as if he'd been expecting him.

"Afternoon, Commissioner Harbaugh. I'm here to—"

"I know why you're here, and I have no comment." Harbaugh opened the door. He wore an ash-grey terry robe over a plain white t-shirt and sweats. "But what's done is done. Might as well come in." He walked off, leaving the door open behind him. Ray entered. Harbaugh poked his head into the foyer from around the corner and pointed to a mat on the floor. "Shoes." Ray obliged, leaving his beat-up black leather cowboy boots beside the door.

Hesitatingly, he followed in his sockfeet from the foyer to a living room lined by potted ferns and framed oil paintings of barns, farms, and landscapes. Past a granite-topped breakfast bar, Ray could see into a spacious kitchen, where a grey-headed woman in white sat at the kitchen table beside a portly nurse who raised a spoonful of soup to the old woman's mouth, gently encouraged her to receive the food, and watched carefully as she swallowed. Her eyes, bright but unfocused, circled aimlessly until they landed on Ray.

"Oh, hi," she smiled. "Who are you?"

"This is Raymond Reynolds," Harbaugh answered before Ray could. "He's a… friend from work."

The woman nodded, a wide smile splitting her face in two. "I'm Barbara," she said to Ray. "Do you want to have lunch with me?"

"Oh, I, uh…" Ray stammered, but the woman looked away as he tried to answer. She turned back to him and smiled again.

"Hi! …who are you? I'm Barbara."

Ray looked at Harbaugh, who sat now on the couch with his hands folded in front of his face. "Chris?" The nurse looked at him. "Can you take Barb and give us a moment? We need to talk privately. Business, you know." The nurse nodded, stood from the table, and helped Barbara to her feet. She followed the nurse, led gently by the arm, down the hall into the recesses of the home. Ray sat opposite Harbaugh, removed his hat, and laid it beside him. Harbaugh lowered his hands and folded them in his lap, frowning at Ray.

"This can be off the record, I hope."

Ray nodded. "So, Barbara, is she…?"

"My wife."

"After Eleanor?"

Harbaugh looked down, smiled darkly to himself. "Shoulda

figured you'd met her. Probably came to you even." He looked back up at Ray, who said nothing. "It's okay. I understand. Part of her never moved on after the divorce. That's her right, I suppose. Did a lot of wrong by her."

"Commissioner—"

"Allen, please."

"...Allen, I'm sorry, but that's not what I'm here about."

The commissioner sighed and nodded. "I know. I got your messages. Maybe I just wanted to think the problem would go away if I ignored it." He shook his head. "Guess I'll never learn."

"I know how that goes."

Harbaugh didn't respond. Ray sat there for a moment, employing the old reporter's trick of letting the silence force the subject into speaking, but Harbaugh remained quiet, his brow furrowed contemplatively. Ray squirmed on the cloud-soft cushion, nervously curling and uncurling his toes inside his socks. Still Allen said nothing, staring sadly at the carpet.

Might as well get into it.

"I obtained a number of county records," Ray said, "that near as I can tell, show a *lot* of taxpayer money was overpaid to Harbaugh Construction. Funds that weren't on the invoices the company submitted. Funds that disappeared somewhere. Anything you want to say about what that's all about?"

Harbaugh smiled, but there was no joy in the grin. "What does it look like?"

"Well, it don't look *good*," Ray said. Harbaugh looked up at him, his grey eyes steely and cold. Ray smiled back. "And the public tends to draw their own conclusions."

Harbaugh exhaled from his nose and rested his head against the back of the couch, staring impassively at the ceiling. "'Spose I should call up my attorney at some point."

"Prob-ab-ly," Ray agreed.

Harbaugh leaned forward again, rubbed his face with his hands.

"Do you know what it's like to watch someone die while they're still alive?"

The temperature of the room seemed to drop a few degrees.

Ray nodded slowly. "Yeah," he said, quietly. "I do."

"So you understand?"

Ray said nothing.

"You need to understand. You need to understand what's at stake, what you're doing," Harbaugh said. "You said this is all off the record?" The reporter nodded. "Not that it matters," the commissioner continued, his voice taking on an icy edge, "not that you *care*, but when Barb first started showing signs, forgetting little things, gettin' all confused over nothin', I just wanted to pretend it was gonna be okay. Just a little lie to get through the day."

"Sure. I tell a few myself."

"But it kept getting worse, until the truth became bigger than the lie. I had to do something." Harbaugh gazed desperately, almost pleadingly, at Ray. "So I did. Alright? I did what I had to do. Who are you to tell me what I should've done?"

"I'm just trying to tell the truth?" Ray shrugged. "And I'm sorry about Barbara. Really, I am. But what do you want from me, just don't publish the story?"

"*Well*," he raised his empty, well-calloused hands, "Your words."

"Look, this is *public* money. And a shit ton of it."

Harbaugh leaned back, crossed his legs, and looked down the long hall Barbara and the nurse had disappeared down. His eyes grew red and wet. Ray wondered if they were crocodile tears on his behalf.

"I'm sorry." Ray hunched over, shaking his head. "But I'm publishin' the story."

Harbaugh, his cheeks flushed, wiped sweat from his brow, despite the humming of the air conditioner in the window. "I'm sure we could… come to some kind of *arrangement*." He smiled a little too wide. "Make it worth your while…"

Ray actually took a second to think about all the things in his life that were always nearly empty: his bank account, his gas tank, his stomach. For a moment, he almost considered it. But instead, he shook his head.

"You ain't got nothin' for me," Ray said.

"But," Harbaugh's lips began to tremble, but his voice was steady and sharp, "think about what'll happen to Barb if *you*—"

"*Me*? You want to lay this on me?" Ray snapped back. "*You* made your choices. Not me. See how that works? You knew what you were doing."

Harbaugh's lips quit their trembling and anger flashed in his eyes. "This is the problem with you people," he said. "Never taking responsibility for the lies you tell, the agendas you push. The *lives* you *ruin*."

"Ohohoho*kay*," Ray genuinely laughed. "It's like that. Alright. The only *lie* I'd be telling is if I let this sleeping dog alone." He stood up, grabbing his hat from the cushion beside him. "And the only mistakes I'm responsible for are *mine*. Tell you what, I've made more of 'em than I've had hot dinners and I carry 'em around like a goddamn albatross 'round my neck every damn day. So you better lawyer up and learn to blame yourself, cause I don't need the weight of your fuck-ups too."

They smoldered at each other for a long, quiet moment, Harbaugh still sitting and Ray standing, their arms both crossed. Harbaugh rose to his full height, all the way to Ray's nose, sneering.

"Get the hell out of my house."

"You got it," Ray said, donning his Stetson. "Thanks for your help with the story."

The sound of Barbara's laughter echoed from down the hall. Harbaugh looked toward the sound, the lines of his face softening instinctively. Ray made for the door but kept slipping as he hurriedly tried to pull on his boots. Harbaugh came into the foyer as Ray was sitting on the floor, awkwardly yanking his pull-straps. Ray stood up, trying to play it cool, and reached for the handle.

"Who was it?" Harbaugh said.

"Wha?"

"You said you knew what it was like. To watch someone die, still living."

Ray stood quiet and still as a statue.

"Who was it?"

He opened the door, stepped through, and pulled it closed behind him as he left.

Back in his Bronco, Ray sat silently for a long time, not smoking, not moving, not thinking. He eventually pulled a joint from his glove box and lit up as he opened his laptop and pulled up the latest version of the article. He added a single line to the end: "When contacted, Harbaugh declined to comment." He fired off the story.

Ray closed the laptop and tossed it into the passenger seat. He thought, for the first time in a long time, about his mother. How her mind and her memory had started to visibly deteriorate before he'd even finished high school, despite how his dad pretended nothing was wrong. How Ray never came back home after joining the Navy, unable to bear the thought of what he might return to. How he wasted all those years following his discharge by drinking and drugging and rambling around the country, without so much as a phone call home to see how she was doing. And how, by the time he finally came back home, the chance had passed forever — just one more in an endless line of regrets that followed Ray through the long, languid years of his life like a shadow.

He rubbed his bloodshot eyes. When had he started crying?

By the time he got back to his apartment, Ray had navigated himself back to a comfortable and familiar emptiness. A reply was waiting in his inbox from his editor. Apparently, the story was too long. She wanted him to cut it down to twenty column inches.

Ray sighed and lit up a joint.

DOWN TO THE KNUCKLE

As the weight shifted in his pocket, Kaczynski knew he was fucked.

He never should've accepted Detective Jameson's offer. Bastard was as crooked as his own teeth. Soon as that plainclothes prick sprung for joint fancy enough to have valet parking and a coat check, he should've seen it as a warning sign, not an olive branch. Too late now. Whatever Jameson paid the staff to slip into the inside pocket of his oversized winter coat was there now, and it couldn't be good. Not something he'd want to examine on the middle of the bus heading out of Center City. He shifted nervously the whole way into Kensington, sizing up the unknown object by feel. A few pounds, softish, rectangular. He chewed the first knuckle on his left hand, an old habit he never got around to breaking.

Goddammit. He never wanted to rat on anyone. Detective Jameson had sought *him* out, promising money, drugs, and warm meals. The three things he always wanted and took whenever he could get. Why had he fucked up a good thing and gone crying to the gang about it?

He gnawed nervously at the knuckle.

He knew the answer, of course. Always had. Reminded himself constantly. He was a chickenshit. A coward. A real piece of shit.

Wanted everything the cops could give him, without having to give up his protection by the Kings. What's the point of cake if you can't eat it too, right?

And now, classic Kaczynski, he'd been playing both sides, feeding a more-or-less equal blend of truth and fiction to each, ultimately endearing him to neither and making him a liability to both. He could've guessed that would happen, but he'd kept pushing the thought to the back of his addled brain. Just one more in a lifetime of problems delayed until the bill came due.

He tasted iron on his tongue and looked down. Blood dripped from his knuckle down his wrist.

He got off three stops before Kings territory began, ducked down a side alley overgrowing with twisting ivory, and removed a book-sized manila package from his coat. With trembling fingers, he opened it. Inside were dozens of bags of prepackaged white powder he couldn't readily ID. Amphetamines? Opiates? They sure as hell weren't powdered sugar. And, more importantly, they weren't his.

These goods were packaged for sale. Jameson knew he wasn't a mover. He wasn't a product guy. He was an information guy. He watched the blocks, kept tabs both sides thought he was keeping on the other, and reported back. If Jameson had wanted him to get something moved, he would've just told him. Not planted it on him. Now somebody would want this shit back, and Jameson, that two-faced motherfucker, knew just where to point them.

This wasn't business. This was murder.

For all Kaczynski knew, maybe the cop had lifted these from one of the King's rivals. Was Jameson trying to set off a turf war?

He moved on to gnawing the second knuckle.

What was his play here? Just toss the drugs? No, he'd be fucked. They were his only leverage, and if the rightful owners found him, they'd kill him.

Come clean to the boss and throw himself on the mercy of the Kings? No, he'd be fucked. They'd rough him up, make an example out of him for the fresh blood, then put a bullet through his head in an empty lot.

Do some of the drugs?

Well, it'd be a start.

He made a little pyramid of snowy powder in his palm. There were two likelihoods, he figured. Either it was cocaine, which just might give him that little bit of extra grit to get through this shit. Or it was fentanyl, and suddenly none of this would be his problem anymore. He weighed dying deep down in an opiate overdose against bleeding out in a gutter.

Kaczynski ripped the powder from his palm.

A nasal drip of chemical aftertaste stained the back of his throat. Uncertain seconds ticked by. He waited for the scales to tip one way or the other. Light and sound took on a hard edge. A wave of spastic mania hit him like a car.

He smiled. It was cocaine.

His first break all damn day. He scampered down the alley, stuffing the package back into his coat.

He needed to stay on the move. No way of telling when the inevitable shit would hit the proverbial fan. Good thing they hadn't taken his boots when they took his coat at the restaurant. The rosewood handle of his .9mm Sig Sauer still dug into his ankle, stuffed into his sock. He moved at a brisk jog parallel to Kings territory, through disputed streets none of the factions had the balls to openly patrol.

Jameson thought he was just some street trash that he could throw away? Son-of-a-bitch thought he could just get rid of him, just like that? Kaczynski smacked his bloody-knuckled fist into his palm. Time for a rude fucking awakening. Unlike Jameson, he didn't mind getting his hands dirty. Jameson had underlings, bootlickers, and bloodsuckers to do his work for him. But Kaczynski had grown up knowing, at the end of the day, the only person he could rely on was himself.

He pulled his phone from the pocket of his tattered jeans and dialed the precinct secretary's personal cell.

"Goddammit, pick up… pick up… answer the fucking phone, I swear to God." He moved onto grinding his teeth atop the knuckle of his ring finger. The line on the other end opened.

"Sandra, listen to— Sandra, I don't care if you can't talk right now, it's an emergency."

He circled around the knuckle bone with his teeth.

"Yes! An actual emergency! I need to talk to Jameson again."

He rolled his dilated eyes.

"I *know* I just talked to him at our meeting today. That's why I said *again*."

A group of guys drinking tallboys around a stoop shot him a dirty look from across the street. Paranoia pounded in his chest and he took a sudden turn down the next alley.

"The kinda shit I can't talk about over the phone, Sandra! Big info, breaking news, just came in, can't wait to go through the usual channels… *Yes*, that means I can't tell you."

He took his frustration out on a trashcan as he passed, scattering hot garbage across the asphalt. A wide woman emerged screaming from a back door and he took off running.

"What? Oh, that? Nothin'. Look, please Sandra, just let me know somewhere I can pop in and talk to Jameson, just five minutes. I can make it worth your while."

He cracked a cocky smile, blood seeping from the broken skin around the knuckle down his chin.

"Yeah, baby, you know I can always get some of that good shit for you. Got some on me right now, as it happens. I'll drop it in the usual spot for ya… just need something from you."

He jumped up and down impatiently.

"Yes! It's good! It's the good shit! Goddamnit, Sandra, time is of the goddamn essence!"

Still she dallied, and he punched the nearest wall, leaving a bloody first print on the brick.

"Sandra, please, I'm sorry… *yes*, I'm sorry for yelling, this is just some fucking *critical* info I can't trust with anyone but Jameson, and

I need to—" She interrupted with an address. "Chuck E. Cheese?" He laughed but choked on his extra saliva. "Why the fuck?"

He blinked several times.

"He has kids? ...*Twins!?*"

He shook his head, turned around, and started running. That was all the way in Northeast Philly. He'd never make it in time on foot.

"No, no, it's just that I didn't think the limey bastard had it in him, is all. Thanks Sandra, I appreci— Yes! It's the good shit! It'll be at the usual spot! Goddammit!"

He hung up, stopped by a rusty red '91 Civic, looked up and down the street, and broke through the window with his Sig. Then he hot-wired the old rustbucket and made for the 95, speeding up alongside the Delaware River, his pistol riding shotgun in the passenger seat. He moved on to chewing his pinky knuckle, the rest of the hand too raw and bloody to keep gnawing. He sideswiped the neighboring car swerving into a parking spot. Airlines screamed overhead, coming and going from the airport across the avenue. He snorted another bump of coke before grabbing his gun.

The gaunt, twitching figure stalked through the parking lot toward the children's restaurant.

Flashing lights, blaring arcade machines, and the cacophony of screaming brats assaulted him as he crossed the threshold of the children's casino. "Can I help you, sir?" asked some pimple-faced teen in a red vest. Kaczynski pushed past him and hopped the turnstile into the arcade, one hand caressing the gun in his pocket. "Sir? Sir!"

Torrents of waddling toddlers and screeching prepubescents ran wild around him as he scanned the arcade for Jameson's oil-black high-and-tight fade, his wide shoulders and fat paunch, his thick forearms ending in meaty fists the size of Kaczynski's head. There he was. Across the sea of children, the bastard sat a table in the dining room surrounded by children and fellow parents, pizza, and luminescent aluminum balloons. Two chubby little Jamesons, a brother and sister with the same wide-set eyes and greasy hair, ripped colorful paper from their presents.

Kaczynski tightened his hands around the rosewood grip and steamed forward, knocking children to the floor in his hurry.

"Jameson, you fucking pig!"

Jameson snapped to his feet, instinctively raising his arms in front of his children. Fury gleamed in his muddy green eyes.

"You better back up, Kaczynski," he hollered. "You better back *way* the fuck up."

Kaczynski pulled the gun from his pocket with his mangled hand. At the sight of the weapon, the arcade erupted, children screaming bloody murder and running every which way. But the little Jamesons didn't run, instead cowering behind their father, gripping his khakis in fat little fists and screaming in full-throated terror.

Kaczynski had the shot. Clear line of sight. Jameson still half a second away from his sidearm. Just pull the trigger. But the little Jamesons' stares ripped through all the light and noise. He knew they'd be here. He knew he'd have to take this shot.

But somehow, classic Kaczynski, he hadn't really thought about it. Just one more thing he'd pushed to the back of his mind. One more bill he figured he'd pay when it came due.

Kaczynski blinked. Blood dripped from his knuckles to the floor. Jameson had reached his gun. The cop bared his mouthful of crooked teeth like an angry dog.

Goddammit. He was fucked.

Jameson emptied the clip into Kaczynski's chest. He collapsed to the floor. The dirty cop walked slowly up to where he lay gasping for air, blood filling his mutilated lungs, and kicked the gun from his teeth-marked hand.

"You know, Kaczynski?" Jameson shook his head. "You're a real piece of shit."

He'd never felt so cold. Even the warmth of the cocaine faded, seeping from his chest to stain the neon-colored carpeting. Was this what dying felt like?

Kaczynski closed his eyes, not wanting Jameson's grinning mug to be the last thing he saw. He tried to bring his knuckles to his mouth, to feel the bone grind beneath his teeth one more time.

Jameson put his boot over Kaczynski's wrist.

WOLF IN WOLF'S CLOTHING

For my friend, Guardian Drake

"Nazi punks fuck off!"
—Dead Kennedys

Raymond Reynolds looked over at the redhead about twelve years his junior sitting in his passenger seat, wearing a full-body fox costume of fire-orange fur. He affectionately stroked the oversized fox head sitting in his lap and smiled back at Ray.

"You sure you're cool?"

Ray, by contrast, wore flannel over a Willie Nelson t-shirt, cowboy boots under mud-stained jeans, and a black flat-top Stetson.

"Yeah, Johnny." Ray puffed on a half-dead joint and passed it over. "I'm always cool."

"Alright." Johnny inhaled, donned his fox head, and exhaled. Smoke leaked through the eyeholes. "Prepare thyself."

They entered the Philadelphia Conference Center Hotel, where Ray was one of relatively few people dressed like, uh… people. Many wore anthropomorphized animal costumes Johnny had informed him were called "fursuits" — wolves and huskies with dopey smiles, kangaroos with functional pouches, horses with flowing manes, even birds and dragons with neon-colored feathers and scales. Even those without full suits often wore animal accoutrement, like ears or fluffy tails.

"Having second thoughts yet?" Johnny asked.

"This was the only way I could afford a room."

"You don't think this is weird?"

"Oh, it's weird as hell," Ray laughed. "But why should that matter?"

Ray turned to look at a commotion in one corner of the hall, where a German Shepherd dressed in black leather waved a picket sign: "Support freedom of speech in the furry community!" The dog wore a red armband with a black pawprint in a white circle, with SS insignia on his lapels.

"Uh, Johnny?" Ray pointed. "The fuck am I looking at?"

"Ugh." He could hear the disgust in Johnny's voice. "RommelDog. Local Nazifur."

"Hol' up," Ray reeled. "Are you telling there are fucking furry *Nazis?*"

"There's shitheads in all walks of life," Johnny said. "Furries love everyone! Furrydom is all about bringing people *together.* That guy? He's like a bug. Just ignore him, and he'll go away."

"But that's not how you deal with bugs? You need, like, ant traps or something…"

"You're missing the point. Just don't pay him any atten—"

A gunshot cut his sentence short. Panicked screams filled the hall to the ceilings. Ray, on instinct, tackled his friend to the floor.

He looked up to see a black bird pointing a handgun at the Nazi dog. A second shot rang out. The dog leapt for cover. The bird turned tail and took flight, pushing through the crowd and escaping into the parking lot. The Nazifur stumbled in the other direction, disappearing into the stampede.

Ray stuck around to give a statement to the police. From what he could overhear, no one saw the shooter enter the lobby — a crow, according to most witnesses.

"A murder of crow!" laughed one of the two cops taking reports.

"So you think you can catch the guy?" Ray asked.

"Guy? I thought we were looking for a bird."

"Don't worry," chuckled his partner. "We'll get animal control right on it."

Back in their room, Ray found Johnny in his boxers smoking a bowl in the bathroom. He'd turned the shower to full blast at max heat to let the steam capture the sticky-sweet smell of weed.

"This is bad, man," Johnny said.

"No one got hurt." Ray took the pipe and filled his lungs with smoke. "Not even by a ricochet. Minor miracle, considering how crowded that hall was."

"What'd the police say?"

"Let's just say I got the feelin' it ain't their highest priority."

"Of course. Fuckin' pigs."

"Hey, isn't that offensive?"

Johnny tilted his head. "To… cops?"

"No, to, like… pig furries?"

Johnny laughed. "You got a good heart, Ray." But his smile disappeared as he checked a notification on his phone.

"What's wrong?"

"The Council of Elderfurs has called a meeting."

Ray waited for Johnny to laugh, not believing there was such a thing, but Johnny stared at him with solemn, bloodshot eyes.

"Wait, are you serious?"

He was serious. That afternoon, all the furries gathered in the hotel auditorium. At a table on the stage, illuminated by spotlight, sat a racoon, a lion, an eagle and a bear, all of them wearing ceremonial velvet robes. Ray, who had smoked three more bathroom bowls, stood rubbing his eyes, mystified by the entire proceeding.

"Take your hat off," Johnny hissed, back in his foxsuit. "Show some respect."

Ray obliged.

"This precious con," declared the raccoon from the stage, "is supposed to be a time of harmony and celebration, when we come together as ourselves. But how can we, when violence has ripped our peace asunder?"

"With all due respect, my esteemed councilor," boomed the bear, "how can we speak of 'peace' and 'harmony' when we allow

RommelDog at our con to begin with? He brings his vile ideology here, and violence comes with it."

"How dare you!" howled a voice from the crowd. The German Shepherd in fascist regalia forced his way onto the stage. "An attempt was made on *my* life on *your* watch, and you blame *me*? I'm the victim here!"

A chorus of angry jeers rose from the crowd.

"Oh, boo yourselves!" the dog barked. "All I wanted is the same rights as everyone else, to be myself at the con, but the Elderfurs tried to censor me! And now someone's tried to censor me for good — but I will not be silenced!"

"Quiet child!" screeched the eagle. "You dare interrupt our deliberations? We will investigate and decide the appropriate course of action!"

"You can't be trusted to investigate! This was a political assassination!" The Nazi climbed onto the table and thrust a fist into the air. "We're all different species, but there's only one master race! Don't trust the Elderfurs!"

The Elderfurs and RommelDog yelled at each other for several minutes. Only a promise from the council to appoint an unbiased party to investigate prompted the Nazi to climb down from the table, but he still refused to leave the stage.

"Who among us could possibly be unbiased?" growled RommelDog. "Who could be trusted to investigate?"

Johnny's eyes lit up underneath his fox head. "Oh! Oh!" He grabbed Ray's arm and pushed through the crowd, pulling him to the stage. "Ray can do it! Ray can solve the case!"

"Wait — wha?"

Before his pot-muddled brain could catch up with what was happening, Ray found himself foisted onstage in front of thousands of furries, all staring at him expectantly with big, plastic eyes.

"What business have you at our con?" asked the raccoon.

"None, really?" Ray pointed at Johnny beside the stage. "I'm just splittin' a room with my buddy so I can see Old Crow Medicine Show? At the Fillmore tomorrow?"

"And what experience do you have as an investigator?" said the bear.

"Again, none, really?"

"He's an investigative reporter for our hometown newspaper!" yelled Johnny. "Last month, a county commissioner stepped down 'cause Ray found out he was embezzling!"

"*Okay*, sure," Ray shrugged, "but c'mon, I ain't up to solvin' no attempted murder."

"Didn't you tell me you once solved a hobo murder aboard a speeding train?"

"I mean, you solve *one* murder…"

"Or that time you solved your friend's murder when you first came back to Haroldston?"

"Technically," Ray demurred, "that one was manslaughter, *so…*"

"Or how about that time you outwitted the Nashville Mafia?"

"Johnny, *please* stop making me sound like I know what I'm doing."

RommelDog pounded a paw against the table. "You know nothing of our community! How could we possibly trust an outsider?"

Ray was more than happy to not get involved, but Johnny leapt onstage and offered to serve as his intermediary to the furry community. The council, seemingly swayed despite RommelDog's objections, nodded as one.

"Go forth," they bowed in unison to Ray. "And seek the truth."

Ray rubbed his eyes and rolled down off the stage, wondering how the hell something like this always seemed to happen to him. The crowd parted like the Red Sea as he sauntered toward the exit. Johnny followed.

"The fuck have you gotten me into?" Ray asked Johnny, back in the lobby. "I swear, if I miss that concert, I will *freak out*."

"Ray, this is serious." Johnny's voice trembled. "I know this all seems like just a bunch of dumb bullshit to you, but this community was here for me when no one else was, y'know? And I just… I don't wanna see it…"

Ray sighed. "Okay, okay, goddammit. Hey." He placed a hand on Johnny's shoulder. "Cheer up, huh? Ole Ray's on the case."

"And *what* a comfort that is," growled RommelDog, appearing from nowhere and inserting himself into the conversation. "This two-bit hick here to see some backwoods jug blowers is gonna figure out who tried to *murder me*."

"Backwoods jug blowers?" Ray gasped. "They're in the Grand Ole goddamn Opry, you racist-ass, jackboot-wearing motherf—"

"I think what Ray's *trying* to say," Johnny inserted himself between them, "is that it's in *everyone's* best interest to try and figure out what happened."

"So then," RommelDog said, "you wanna take my statement, or what?"

"Man, I ain't the police." Ray rolled his bloodshot eyes. "So get outta my face."

"Wow. Such professionalism. You don't even want to ask if I have any enemies?"

"You're a fuckin' Nazi. So I assume… everyone?"

"See? I told the council you couldn't be trusted!"

"Jesus Christ." Ray rubbed his temples. "Fine. Do you have any enemies?"

"As a matter of fact…" The German Shepherd wrapped a leather arm around his shoulders. "Now that you mention it, there's one person comes to mind." He leaned in close enough that Ray could smell his breath, even through the doghead. "Bellow, he goes by now. The deer."

Johnny's shoulders tightened. "Bellow?"

"Everyone knows he doesn't want me to be part of this community. Now it looks like he's tried to keep me out, permanently."

Ray ducked out of his embrace. "And that's jus' you spitballin'?"

"No, it's more than that." His voice took on an icy edge. "The bastard tried to shoot me was wearing a crow suit. Everyone knows Bellow's old fursona was a crow, 'fore he got that fancy new suit."

"That's true…" Johnny said softly. "But I remember hearing Bellow couldn't come to the con this year. So how could he have—"

"You believe that? I bet he only *said* that so no one would *expect* him. Then he comes here in his *old* suit so people won't think it's him, and…" He made a finger gun with one of his paws. "Blam."

Ray looked to Johnny, who stared back at him with plastic eyes.

"Alright," Ray sighed. "I guess we'll look into it."

"Great," the dog growled, walking away. "I feel safer already."

Ray watched him go. "The hell is *with* that guy?"

"People like that, there's nothing to them," Johnny said. "He's a troll. All he cares about is saying dumb shit and getting under people's skin."

Ray could hear a twinge in his voice. "He gettin' under yours?"

"It's just… I know Bellow. We had a, uh, *liaison* at his place during last year's con."

"What do you mean, a liaison?"

Johnny blushed beneath his fox head. "A lady doesn't kiss and tell, Ray."

Ray chuckled. "Good for you."

They burned down a joint in Ray's truck on the drive over to Bellow's apartment. He wasn't home, but his roommate, a young guy about Johnny's age, let them come inside. The whole place reeked of weed.

"Any idea where he is?" Ray asked. "It's an emergency."

"Are you two cops?" His eyes were bloodshot and paranoid.

"Do we *look* like cops?" Ray gestured between himself and Johnny, still in his foxsuit. "Besides, even if we were, you know we don't gotta tell you? That's just some bullshit on TV."

Ray smiled at him like a dentist at a mouthful of cavities.

The guy gave up an address.

They ended up outside a well-built Georgian house on a manicured lawn in an upscale neighborhood. A dozen vehicles were parked in front of the house as Ray and Johnny rolled up, a personal cloud of smoke swirling inside their cabin.

A woman with silver hair and a black dress answered when they rang the bell. She looked back and forth between the cowboy-lookin' fella and the cartoonishly proportioned bipedal fox standing on her porch, clutching a tissue to her breast.

"Can I help you?"

"We're looking for Bel—"

"Paul," Johnny interrupted him. "We're looking for Paul."

She furrowed her brow and retreated. A few moments later, a young man with heavy brows in a black suit appeared in the doorway.

"Foxtrot?" he said. "The hell are you doing here?"

"We're here on behalf of the council," Johnny said.

"I don't care! My family doesn't know I'm into all this, okay? And you come here, in your fursuit, while we're sitting shiva for my Aunt Meribeth?"

Ray blinked. "Sitting… shiva?" He noticed the kippah hat Paul wore on the back of his scalp, and the black mourning band around his arm. "Ah, *shit…*"

"What?" Paul demanded.

"Someone tried to shoot RommelDog," Johnny said.

"And, uh," Ray winced, "he said it mighta been you?"

"And you believed him?" His face flushed with anger. "He's a fucking Nazi!"

"Look, I'm not sayin' that ain't an excellent point," Ray said. "But he said the shooter was the same kinda bird you like to dress as?"

"I shouldn't even have to dignify that with a response, but I *sold* that suit online last year so I could afford my new deer suit? And, I don't know if I've mentioned, but I've kind of been busy? Mourning my dead aunt? So, as much as that anti-Semitic motherfucker might *deserve* it, I haven't been able to pencil shooting him into my busy schedule." He shot a bitter glare at Johnny. "See you around, Foxtrot."

And with that, he slammed the door in their faces. They drove back toward the hotel, both of their faces burning with embarrassment.

"You didn't mention he was Jewish," Ray said after a while.

"I didn't realize," Johnny muttered. "We didn't really do much *talking* that night, I guess…"

Ray frowned to himself. Something about the whole strange affair just didn't seem right. He had *seen* the second shot — the bird had been only a few feet away, dead to rights, and *still* missed. Then, miraculously, no one got hit by a stray *or* a ricochet. *Then* the Nazi goes out of his way to make them think it was a Jewish member of the community who'd pulled the trigger.

The whole thing just seems too goddamn convenient…

"Unless…" Ray snapped his fingers.

Johnny tilted his head. "Unless what?"

"Unless there *were no* gunshots."

"What?"

"Shut up and come on," Ray said, pulling in at the hotel. "I have a hunch."

Ray told the front desk he lost his keycard.

"I know this sounds crazy," he said, "but I… left it? In my other kangaroo pouch?" He cleared his throat. "Which was *stolen*."

"Sir, I've worked this convention the last four years," the concierge said. "Nothing sounds crazy to me anymore. What room?"

Ray smiled. "1488, I think."

Upstairs, Ray swiped the ill-gotten keycard. The door unlocked. Sure enough, the personal effects tossed over the bed were decorated with Nazi imagery.

"Woah," Johnny said. "How'd you know this was his room?"

"Nazis like the numbers 14 and 88, right? There's no room 14, there's no room 88, there's no room 8814…"

They searched through RommelDog's belongings but found no crow suit, and no gun. Ray knelt in front of the hotel safe in the closet. It needed a four digit code. 1488? The lock buzzed red. 8814? The lock buzzed red.

"Wait, dude," Johnny leaded in over his shoulder. "I have an idea."

He pressed one, one, one… one. The lock clicked green.

Johnny laughed maniacally.

Ray shook his head. "Dumbass fascist fuckheads, I swear to God…"

Inside the safe, a fursuit of black synthetic feathers was folded beneath a Colt .380. Ray inspected the pistol. It was missing two rounds, and the remaining rounds were all blanks.

"Motherfucker…" Ray breathed.

"Oh shit," Johnny said. "Wait. What does this mean?"

"It means, this whole thing was just some racist false-flag bullshit."

"No, what this means," came a voice behind them, "is you've actually done me a huge favor."

Ray and Johnny turned to find RommelDog, clapping his paws together in mocking applause.

"I got to say, *thank you* for breaking the law like this," the Nazi laughed. "You realize none of this is admissible in court now, right?"

Ray laughed, a high-pitched stoner's giggle.

"What?" RommelDog barked. "What's funny?"

"Remember what I told you?" Ray approached, holding the pistol by the barrel. "I told you, I ain't the police."

"So?"

"So get outta my face."

Ray drew his arm back, and cracked RommelDog across the jaw with the handle of the gun. The Nazi crumpled to the floor.

"Holy *shit*, dude!" Johnny put his paws to his snout. "You fucking pistol-whipped him!"

"Yeah, but…" Ray shrugged. "He's a fuckin' Nazi?"

That very night, the Council of Elderfurs voted to exile RommelDog. Stripped of his fursuit, the convention-goers cheered as police led him through the hotel lobby in handcuffs.

"I've been framed!" he screeched, scrawny and pockmarked outside of his suit. "It's a conspiracy against me! You've gotta believe me!"

"It's a dog-eat-dog world, huh?" chuckled one cop.

"Don't worry," laughed his partner. "Maybe PETA will represent you."

Ray and Johnny watched from Ray's truck, smoking a celebratory joint as the crowd burned RommelDog's suit in effigy in the parking lot.

"You done good, Ray," Johnny coughed.

"No." Ray frowned. "There's still one out there."

"What?"

"There has to be. Someone was in RommelDog's costume, someone pulled the trigger in the crow suit. There's another Nazi out there somewhere, hiding. Like a rat."

"Dude, that's offensive."

Ray titled his head. "To… Nazis?"

"No, to rat furries."

"Oh. Sorry."

"Hey, cheer up, alright?" Johnny laid a hand on his shoulder. "I mean it, you done good. Even if there's more out there. It's like you said, when you got bugs, you put out ant traps."

Ray squinted at his friend, having totally forgotten this conversation.

"Wait — wha?"

REAL MAGIC

Robert Falsch stood onstage admiring the gilded interior of the Forrest Theatre, an opulent palace of a venue illuminated by a crystal chandelier of dazzling size. Located in Philadelphia's Center City, the auditorium boasted nearly 2,000 plush maroon seats, frequently filled by some of the city's most successful collectors of wealth and power.

"This is the perfect place for a fresh start," Falsch said. "Even a couple easy marks in a place like this will net us a hefty score."

Falsch — a lanky figure approaching middle age with thin, almost translucent skin, wearing a twin-tailed velveteen suit and feathered homburg hat — turned to his partner Cera Dieben, a serious woman in her mid-twenties. Even the bedazzled leotard couldn't brighten her expression.

"I don't know, Bobby," she said, the doubt in her hazel eyes concealed behind her favorite gold-plated aviators. "After what happened in San Francisco, isn't this gig still a little too soon?"

"Cera, we talked about this. Call me Byron. I need to get into my new character."

"But Bobby—"

He held up a finger. "Byron Davenport, the bewitching!"

She sighed. "I'm being serious, *Byron*. The heat's still after us. I know we changed the name of the act, but are you really sure that's gonna be enough this time?"

"Ah, but of course," Falsch exclaimed, tossing and rolling his hat down his arm. "For Byron Davenport is a defier of the impossible, one who bends life and death, space and time, to his will through mastery of forbidden knowledge!" He popped the hat with his elbow, caught it by the brim, and reached inside to produce a crimson rose. "Surely the laws of men are nothing compared to the laws of reality! Don't you believe in me?"

"Depends on which one of you is asking," Cera said. "I *believe* in Bobby Falsch, the nimblest fingers to ever prestidigitate. And *he* always knew when to keep quiet once we'd attracted too much attention to ourselves."

With a twirl of his wrist, the rose vanished again. "Cera, we're in a new city, on a new coast, under a new name," he insisted. "It's just like what we do in our act. Keep the audience's attention where you want it, and you can do whatever you please anywhere they're not looking."

"I suppose…"

"Do you *really* think I'm the nimblest fingers in the game?"

"Of course I do! Why the fuck else would I have stuck it out with you this long?"

"Then *trust me*. I know San Francisco was a bust, a big one. But our luck is about to change."

Cera allowed her reservations to melt into a gentle smile. "Alright, Bobby — I mean, *Byron*. I'm with you." She struck a dramatic pose. "Where would a magician be without his fabulous assistant?"

"In my case?" Falsch laughed. "Probably in jail."

She laughed too. "Just so long as you remember that."

• • •

They say that one's own left hand can never know the actions of the right. So if an audience is focused on a performer's right, how could they possibly notice what's left? And when Bobby Falsch and Cera Dieben would finish their routine, a select few audience members would find that *nothing* was left. Cash, credit cards, jewelry, all gone, disappeared into the magicians' pockets like a rabbit back into a hat.

Back when Falsch was still a solo act performing under the name Marion Carnegie — "the mesmerizing!" — he would simply call an audience member onstage and fleece them of their watch, cufflinks or earrings while they were picking trick cards from his deck. More than the money, it was the thrill that drove him: the knowledge that he could take whatever he pleased, while an entire room of onlookers remained oblivious.

That was real magic.

Cera Dieben, a young con and practiced pickpocket, was the first person to ever spot what he was doing. He'd been on tour one summer and had just finished a particularly successful show in Vegas, having pilfered dozens of carats worth of gold jewelry, when he returned to his previously locked dressing room to find her inside, waiting for him.

"You're damn good," she'd told him. "But you could be even better. Every magician needs an assistant, and all the classic cons are two-man jobs."

"Shouldn't you be a man, then?" he'd said. "Besides, the *greats* all work alone."

Then she twirled her fingers to reveal she was wearing each of the gold rings that Falsch had just stolen, which *should've* been secretly secure inside his breast pocket. He couldn't help but smile. They'd worked together ever since, going on nearly four years. He'd never asked why she was so eager to get out of the city, and Cera had never volunteered the information, but the new partnership quickly bore fruit.

Falsch would still pick an audience member or two to call onstage to plunder personally, for love of the craft, but Cera's role was now the real moneymaker, and a deceptively simple one at that. Only a handful of tricks Flasch performed required the help of an assistant, all frontloaded near the start of the act. While Cera was unneeded on stage, she would slip into an usher's uniform and stalk the theater aisles, pulling rings from fingers, watches from wrists, and pocket-books from unattended purses. After all, who pays attention to an usher when the performance they paid to see is still unfolding?

Except for once in San Francisco…

But that night at the Forrest Theatre, all eyes remained locked on "the bewitching Byron Davenport" as a nondescript usher quietly palmed valuables out from beneath the very noses of their owners.

Onstage, the act proceeded as smoothly as it ever had. Falsch stood bound with his hands cuffed behind his back, his entire body encircled by heavy chains secured by padlocks. He balanced atop a stool, with another chain hanging from the ceiling wrapped around his neck, creating a palpable tension as he struggled to maintain his balance while wriggling himself free of his restraints.

The illusion of danger, naturally, was merely that: an illusion. The chain wrapped around his neck was secured with a loop that dangled down his back, out of sight. In the unthinkable event that Falsch bungled the trick, the loop would pass safely over his head and the chain would untangle, leaving him decidedly unstrangled.

Furthermore, the chains themselves posed little challenge for Falsch, who possessed a rare tool in his magical arsenal not shared by most. Thanks to a quirk of genetics, Falsch had been diagnosed at a young age with Ehlers-Danlos syndrome — a disorder of his body's connective tissues, resulting in stretchy, elastic-like skin and joints that could bend and contort well beyond the capabilities of the average person. The handcuffs were as simple as extending his thumb out of its socket, allowing him to slip his hand from the metal ring as easily as from an unbuttoned sleeve. The padlocked restraints merely required that he pull his shoulders far enough out of place to free his arms, at which point gravity would send the chains clattering to the stage.

The trick was to sell it. If the audience felt he could escape, free of danger, what would be the point of watching? And so Falsch teetered to and fro atop his stool, pulling the metal noose taut before reeling himself back into place, savoring the gasps each time he nearly toppled to his presumed doom.

When he finally freed himself of the chains around his torso, cheers rose from the crowd. But in a final twist, Falsch leapt from the stool without unwrapping his neck, prompting the cheers to turn instantaneously to horrified shrieks. In one fluid motion, he pantomimed untying the chain while the hidden loop passed harmlessly over his head. Landing as gracefully as a trained dancer, he took a deep bow. The squeals ruptured back into cheers, louder than before.

From the wings, changing back out of her usher's suit, Cera shot him a quiet thumbs up. Falsch nodded. Time for his favorite part. "For this next trick," he beamed out into the theater, "I'm going to need a volunteer."

Dozens of hands shot up, several of whom would've been easy marks for Falsch's routine. But he already had a target picked out, a gentleman in the front row accompanied by two children of elementary school age wearing coordinated outfits. The mark wore a tailored maroon suit with a boldly patterned shirt beneath, open at the collar to reveal tufts of silver chest hair and a gold chain. Well-built but balding and slightly heavyset, he possessed the figure of a retired athlete: still strong, but growing soft around the middle from fine wines and exotic foods. But the detail that had attracted Falsch's eye was his watch — a solid gold Rolex Yacht-Master II, the watchface encircled by sapphire. A retail value easily upwards of $75,000.

"How about you, sir?" Falsch pointed. The gentleman scowled and raised his hands, demurring. Falsch's smile tightened. He'd picked his target, and he would have his prize.

"Aw, would you look at that, folks?" He turned to the rest of the auditorium. "He's shy! Why don't you all give him a little encouragement?" Obligingly, the theater-goers broke into gentle laughter and applause. Falsch waved his arms, stoking the fires. "Come on, come on, let him hear it!"

Still, the watchbearer shook his head. But Falsch's secret weapon was already at work — the two children, likely grandkids. Overall, he struck Falsch as an overly serious fellow, meaning the children were likely the only reason he was there. And the children, as predicted, were aghast that their grandpa would turn down the opportunity to go onstage at a *real* magic show, with a *real* magician, who does *real* magic. They pulled on his suit sleeves, pleading with him to take part.

"Pop-Pop!" they squealed. "Pop-Pop, *pleeeease!*"

"Join me, sir!" Falsch cajoled. "Wouldn't want to disappoint the children, would we?"

With great reluctance, the mark stood up from his seat. His grandchildren cheered with glee, as did the rest of the audience. He patted the children's heads, but waved his hands dismissively to the rest of the theater, wearing a look of angry annoyance. Falsch noted the hardness of his eyes, the tension of his movements. Whatever he'd done to earn the status symbol on his wrist, it had done a number on him.

But, then again, doesn't it always?

"Wonderful sir, right this way, let me help you up…"

In the same motion with which he'd offered his hand, Falsch reached forward and replaced the mark's Rolex with a cheap knock-off he carried up his sleeve for just such a purpose — nothing that would sustain close inspection, but enough to maintain the illusion until it was too late. From there, the real watch disappeared up Falsch's sleeve, where a slight jimmying landed it safely in his breast pocket. The mark wasn't even onstage and Falsch had already completed his goal. It was disappointing, making the magician reluctant to even bother with the trick, but the show must indeed go on — truly, the theater's greatest tragedy.

While pulling the mark onstage, Falsch planted the card he would need in place for the act, at which point he made an unsettling discovery. The mark was strapped, carrying a sidearm in a shoulder rig beneath his jacket. A big one, by the feel of it. A mankiller.

That had never happened before.

"Alright, alright," the man said in a gruff voice. "Let's get this over with."

Flasch considered possibilities. Maybe he was a cop, which wouldn't be good. But a watch like that, on a civil servant? Unlikely. A highly paid private security contractor seemed equally unlikely. Best case scenario, he was just some white-collar paper pusher who appreciated his right to bear arms a little too much.

Worst case scenario?

Well, probably best not to think about it. Besides, the watch was already in Falsch's pocket, and that's where it was going to stay until it was replaced by a fat wad of cash.

"Hello? We getting this show on the road or what, pal?"

"Of course, sir, of course," Falsch laughed, back in the moment. "Thank you for joining me."

"Yeah, yeah, play your little tricks." The man cracked his knuckles, a thick, heavy sound. "I see straight through your act, buddy."

"Why, sir…" Falsch adopted a practiced smile. "I assure you, this is *real* magic. I'm no trickster, but an artist."

"A *bullshit* artist, maybe." He winked. "I can spot 'em a mile away."

Falsch turned to the audience. "We have ourselves a skeptic, folks!" A chorus of light-hearted boos rose from the crowd. "Look at that, sir. See? They believe in me."

"What's next, you gonna saw me in half? Ask me to pick a card?"

From his empty hands, Falsch suddenly produced a deck of cards. "Would you look at that! Are you sure *you're* not a magician, sir? What clairvoyance!"

The man grumbled. Falsch spread the deck before him, face down.

"Any card?" the mark asked.

Falsch nodded. "Any card." The mark took a card from the far left and examined it. "Got it memorized?"

"What do I look, stupid to you?"

"Not at all, sir. Back in the deck she goes…"

After the card had been replaced (an ace of spades, Falsch knew without doubt), the magician shuffled the cards in airborne arcs from one hand to the other. The crowd giggled, while awe danced across the faces of the boy and the girl in the front row. The mark rolled his eyes and raised his sleeve to check the time on his watch.

Hurriedly, Falsch caught the cards and spread them, shoving them in his face. The mark released his sleeve, letting it cover the knock-off watch.

Falsch sighed inaudibly. He singled one card out from the deck, raising it without touching it.

"Is… *this* your card?"

The mark took one look at the card, a five of hearts, and chuckled smugly. "No, that's not my card at all."

"Are you sure, sir?" Now was Falsch's turn to emit a smug chuckle. "Why don't you look again?" And with that, he flicked the card — transforming it, before everyone's eyes, into the mark's driver license.

The audience cheered. From the front row, the grandchildren brayed like donkeys. The mark's eyes narrowed and he stuck his fingers in his belt loops, sizing Falsch up like a prizefighter.

"Nicholas Tremaglio," Falsch read, spinning the card between his fingers. "Are you having an enjoyable evening at the theater, Mr. Tremaglio?"

"*Tremalio*," he said, through gritted teeth. "The 'G' is silent. But anyone from around here would *know* that."

"My apologies, sir." He extended the license. "Please, have it back, of course…"

Tremaglio snapped the card out of Falsch's hands. He pulled his leather wallet from his breast pocket and opened it to replace his ID card. His face tightened and his shoulders dropped when he saw what was inside.

"What is it, sir?" Falsch said, still beaming. "Is something there?"

Half-heartedly, Tremaglio pulled from the space where he kept his driver's license another card entirely — an ace of spades. The auditorium shook with applause. Falsch bowed. Tremaglio, seemingly sickened by the whole affair, crumpled the card and threw it to the stage. He steamed offstage and let himself back down into the audience. At his seat, his grandchildren giggled and poked him. He shooed them off, a hint of embarrassment heating his cheeks.

Falsch smiled with self-satisfaction.

"Well, Forrest Theatre, I have one more trick for you all this evening…"

Down in the first row, eager to leave, Tremaglio raised his sleeve and checked the hour without intervention. At first, he merely noted the time and let his sleeve drop again.

Falsch exhaled in relief.

But then, half a second later, realization sparked in Tremaglio's eyes and he looked a second time. His face turned purple-red with fury. He slowly brought his gaze back up to Falsch, practically frothing at the mouth.

With the quickness that only comes from instinct honed by practice, Tremaglio's hand traveled under his jacket to his gun, but stopped, as if he had suddenly remembered where he was.

That seemed like Falsch's cue to beat a hasty retreat.

"…and that final trick," Falsch finished addressing the audience, "is the vanishing act."

With that, he dropped one of the two smoke bombs he carried up his sleeves, filling the stage with a sudden rush of opaque purple clouds. Falsch grabbed Cera by the wrist and pulled her at top speed toward the backstage exit. By the time Tremaglio had climbed back up onstage, his hand around the handle of his gun, Falsch and Cera were already back in their van, peeling out of the parking lot.

"The fuck, Bobby?" Cera said. "That's not how the act ends."

"Cera, please," he laughed with feigned nonchalance. "If you can predict the ending, doesn't it cease to be a trick?"

●　●　●

Falsch drove straight to the nearest pawn shop, a place called Wild Wesley's located in a grimier part of town. "Cash fast," advertised a neon sign in the barred window. "No ???'s asked."

Before they got out of the van, Cera grabbed his arm. "Alright Bobby, what's up?"

"What are you talking about?"

"You're acting funny — cutting the act short, driving us out to this rando shop. Why not wait until we can hook up with Vinny to fence the stuff? It'll take longer, sure, but a place like this, we'll be lucky to get twenty percent."

"Trust me," Falsch pulled the Rolex from his pocket. "The sooner we offload *this*, the better."

Cera whistled. "Nice grab. Pulled it off that Tremaglio guy?"

"Indeed, like candy from a baby."

"So what's the problem?"

"Well, he might've, ah… *noticed*…"

"He *might've* noticed? The fuck does that mean?"

"It means, he sat down and looked at his wrist afterward, then he looked back up at me and he looked none too happy." Falsch kept the detail of Tremaglio's gun to himself, though it was certainly a factor in his decision-making. "So, I figure he's gonna report it to insurance, or the cops, or whoever, as soon as he gets home. Meaning we need to offload this *before* the serial number gets flagged, ASAP."

"Seriously, Bobby?"

"Sooner, if possible."

"How could *you*, of all people, get spotted? This is San Francisco all over again!"

"Excuse me?" His voice rose an octave. "San Francisco was *your* fault!"

"*My* fault? Maybe if *someone* could've held the audience's attention, they wouldn't've been looking at the fucking usher!"

"Please, we *cannot* go over this again," he groaned, rubbing his temples. "For now, let's just lose the goods and get lost. I hear Baltimore is on the rise these days…"

"Fine. Whatever." Despite the dark of the evening, she took her golden aviators from the glove box and settled them overtop her nose. "But we better go to the fucking aquarium!"

These were terms Falsch could agree to.

Inside the pawn shop, a greasy character greeted them, with slicked back hair, teeth that were either gold or missing, and a spiderweb tattoo that radiated out from the corner of his left eye. The name "Wes" was stitched into the breast of his bowling shirt. Around him, the walls and counters boasted a phantasmagoria of artifacts sold for a quick buck, everything from military surplus gear, sporting goods, and weaponry to musical instruments and jewelry.

"Welcome to Wild Wesley's," the proprietor gave a cavernous smile. "You buyin', browsin', or sellin'?"

"My good man," Falsch extended his hand, "my name is Byron Davenport; this is my assistant... Olga Haberdasher." Cera glared at him. They hadn't discussed her cover name yet. He paid her no mind. "We have a *wonderful* selection of items that are sure to interest a man of taste and sophistication such as yourself."

The shop owner didn't shake hands. Instead, he hocked a lipful of tobacco juice into a jar on the counter. Some of it missed, splattering on the countertop. Falsch removed his hand, trying not to grimace.

"So which is it?" Wesley asked.

"What?"

"Buyin', browsin' or sellin'?"

Falsch blinked, still wearing his stage smile. "*Selling*. We're selling, sir."

"Why didn't you jus' say so? You dense?"

"Not at all; my apologies, sir..."

Behind him, Cera rolled her eyes. Falsch could already tell he was going to get an earful about this later.

"We got a whole estate's worth of jewelry for you," Cera said, producing the bag of goods. "Good shit, too. Stuff that'll fetch a high price."

Wesley picked through the offerings. "Necklaces... bracelets... earrings..." He spat another tobacco loogie into the jar. "There's, what, six, seven sets of weddin' rings here?" He grinned up at them. "Exactly how many times youse two been married before, huh?"

"My good sir," Falsch grinned right back, "I thought your sign promised no questions asked?"

Wesley laughed like he had something caught in his throat. "Haha! Fair enough, I s'pose, fair enough… I'll give you a thousand for the collection."

"One measly thousand?" Cera elbowed Falsch in the ribs, obviously pissed they weren't going through their usual fence.

"Sir, please," Falsch said. "I understand the purpose of an initial offer, but there's no need to insult us. Besides, you've yet to see the crown jewel of our collection…"

Falsch raised his empty hand, spun his wrist, then closed and reopened his fist. The Rolex magically appeared in his palm. The magician dangled it in front of the shopkeeper's greedy eyes.

"The Rolex Yacht-Master II," Falsch did his best Vanna White impression, stroking the watch with one hand. "Solid 18 carat gold, totally waterproof, complete with a sapphire bezel. The highest echelon of elegance for the sailing man — a retail value of $125,000."

Wes whistled. "It's a pretty thing, I'll give you that."

He reached for the watch to inspect further. Falsch let him take it. He examined the Rolex from various angles. His eyes narrowed at the backside of the watch face.

"What's this inscription here?" Wesley asked. "*For N.T., love Abby.*"

Cera elbowed him again. In his hurry, Falsch had neglected to take a closer inspection. He hadn't known the engraving was there, let alone possessed an explanation of its meaning. Instead, after a moment's hesitation, he said, "Wouldn't that be another of those pesky questions you don't ask?"

Wesley made and held eye contact for a long moment, a serious look on his face. Falsch maintained his smile, belying a nervous tremor in his stomach. Finally, the shop owner burst out laughing again.

"Fair enough, fair enough!" He slapped the countertop. "I do knock off five thousand for each question I don't ask, though." Wesley winked. "Call it a convenience fee."

"Of course, sir," Falsch nodded. "I believe we have an understanding."

"Sure, sure we do..." He looked at the watch again. "Something this nice though, need to dot the I's and cross the T's — weigh it, check the carats. That sort of thing. Only way I can be sure I'm willing to pay such a high price for it."

"Naturally. It's a lovely item. I'm sure you'll be satisfied."

"I got a jeweler's set in the back." He opened a door behind the counter that led into the recesses of the shop. "Why don't youse two step back here, I'll take a quick look and we'll get you on your way, your wallets nice and fat. Sound good?"

Cera elbowed him in the ribs again. Falsch elbowed her back. "Sounds excellent, my good man," he said.

Falsch circled around the counter and ducked through the doorway. Cera reluctantly followed. As soon as their backs faced the shopkeep, Wesley grabbed a baseball bat from a perch on the wall. He brought it down hard across both of their skulls. Falsch hit the floor first. Cera followed him down. As blackness overtook his vision, the sound of Wesley's voice reached Falsch's ears, muted and distant, as if he were underwater.

"Boss, I got something here I think you're gonna wanna see... Couple of asshats dressed like cartoon characters just tried to sell me *your* watch..."

Falsch tried to stand, but his strength had pulled a vanishing act. Darkness enveloped him.

* * *

When Falsch awoke, it was to Cera's voice and a headache that felt like his skull was two sizes too small.

"Bobby!" she hissed. "Jesus Christ, you finally awake? Took you long enough."

"Where…" Falsch opened his eyes, but the outside world was too bright. He shut them again. "Where are we?"

"At the fucking Louvre, contemplating the Mona Lisa's smile."

"Then why does my head hurt?"

"Because your dumb ass couldn't just wait to offload the watch with Vinny!"

Falsch forced his eyes open again, blinking through the brightness until the world came into focus. They were in some dingy storeroom crammed with junk and spiderwebs. Across the room, a set of stairs ascended to a closed door. He attempted to rub his throbbing head, but found that his arms were handcuffed to a study metal chair. So were Cera's. Images began floating back into mind: their act at the Forrest Theatre, the Rolex, Tremaglio realizing he'd been swindled, their hasty escape, Falsch's decision to offload the watch at the first pawn shop on their way out of town…

He groaned, a deep sound of frustrated realization. He wiggled his arms, checking what tools he still had up his sleeves. Either they hadn't patted him down, or they hadn't done it very well, because one smoke bomb still remained hidden up his left sleeve.

"I swear, Bobby, I dunno if you've just been off lately, or if you're not really as good as I thought. But either way, I'm starting to rethink some things."

Falsch guffawed. "Me? I'm *still* the greatest. You're the one who's been slowing us down ever since San Francisco!"

Cera thrashed against her restraints. "Fuck you, Bobby!"

"Look, none of that matters right now. I'll be out of my cuffs in five seconds, and I'll have yours off another ten after that." He started working one hand up through the cuff, stretching his thumb out of place to pass under the metal ring.

"Problem is…" Cera nodded toward the opening door, "I don't think we have fifteen seconds."

Two figures entered and descended: spiderweb-faced Wesley and the man he'd referred to as his boss, Nicholas Tremaglio, still wearing the same maroon suit and furious expression from earlier that evening. Falsch slipped his left hand out of its cuff and caught it before it clattered against the chair.

"Well, well, well," Tremaglio said, clapping disingenuously as he approached. "That was some magic show tonight."

"Ah, sir, thank you kindly," Falsch began, "but I fear there's been some kind of terrible misunder—"

Tremaglio backhanded Falsch across the face. Even such a casual gesture from a man of Tremaglio's physicality carried enormous weight, easily breaking the illusionist's nose. The same condition that enhanced Falsch's escape artistry also left him uniquely vulnerable to injury, and he looked back to his jailer with the entire right side of his face bruised the deep purple of ruptured blood vessels.

"Save the bullshit," Tremaglio said. "And don't even bother trying to get outta here. These ain't the trick cuffs you use in your act."

"I assure you, sir, those restraints were genuine." Falsch couldn't help but smile, still holding the side of the handcuff he'd already escaped. "Everything you saw tonight was *real* magic."

While they spoke, Wesley affixed a lecherous gaze on Cera. He leaned over and stroked her face, chuckling. She leaned back, threatening to lose her balance to escape his touch.

"Wesley, contain yourself," Tremaglio barked over his shoulder. "Show our guests a little respect."

"Guests? Boss, they stole from you. From *you!*"

"*She* didn't. She stole from everyone else. Only *this* one," he gestured to Falsch, "actually stole from *me*. Besides, they ain't from around here. I doubt they even know who I am." Tremaglio stuck his thumbs through his belt loops, opening his jacket enough to expose the butt of his gun. "You two got any idea?"

Falsch did, but he kept his mouth shut. He couldn't take many more hits. If Cera had figured it out, she didn't say anything.

"Let's just say I'm a manager for a very powerful family business," Tremaglio said, voice dripping with the self-assurance of power. "And I got where I am by not taking shit from nobody. You could even say I got it *made*."

"You're in the Mafia," Cera said. "A family man."

She shot Falsch an ugly look of pure contempt. He could read it like a classroom note: *"How the fuck did you not clock that before you pulled him onstage?"* Probably with something like *"you fucking idiot!"* tacked on at the end.

"You know, it's not a bad racket you two got going. Wesley showed me your take from the theater." Tremaglio nodded appreciatively. "One professional to another, you have my respect."

"Look at that!" Falsch cried. "We just got off on the wrong foot!" The gears spun wildly in his head, desperately looking for any way out of this situation. "A pair of skilled hands like us, a man of resources such as yourself — imagine the work we could do together!"

In one practiced motion, Tremaglio pulled his pistol from its holster and shoved it under Falsch's chin. "The work we *could've* done together. I could forgive you comin' into my turf and not payin' your respects. Hell, maybe I could even forgive you for stealin' from me. That's how you earn your livin', and you didn't know any better, now did you?"

"N-no, sir," Falsch gulped. "See? Just a big misunderstanding, that's all."

"But here's the thing." He took a deep breath, and when he spoke again his voice was a pot of anger threatening to boil over. "You embarrassed me in front of my grandkids. *Nobody* embarasses Pop-Pop."

"S-sir, w-w-wait, please, let me make amends," Falsch stammered, improvising. "In my right shoe, you'll find the credit cards from your wallet. At least let me return them to you."

Tremaglio's eyes flickered downward. Behind him, Wesley stood watching with crossed arms, sucking on his tobacco. Falsch, naturally, was lying. There was nothing in his shoes except his socks and feet. But if he could direct Tremaglio's attention for long enough, maybe, just maybe, he could pull off his most impressive escape yet...

But what about Cera?

He glanced sideways at her. Her eyes flitted back and forth

between him and their captors, filled with a mixture of fear, fury, and disgust, at least some of which was directed at him. But why should it be? He'd always done fine for himself as a solo artist. It was *her* who had complicated everything. In fact, if *she* hadn't fucked up San Francisco, they never would've needed to flee the West Coast. So, in a way, wouldn't that make this whole debacle tonight *her* fault?

Falsch made up his mind. After all, don't the greats all work alone?

Tremaglio lowered the gun from Falsch's chin. "Too little, too late," he said. "We would've found them when we were fitting you for concrete shoes."

Despite the threat, that was a good sign. It meant that Tremaglio hadn't inspected his wallet more closely after the show. If he had, he would've known that none of his cards were missing. He believed Falsch's lie, which was the first step.

The trick now was to sell it.

Falsch burst into crocodile tears. "I know it won't change anything," he cried, "but all I've ever done my entire life is steal from other people. At least allow me the grace of returning what I've taken from you while I'm still alive!" Tremaglio tried to respond, but Falsch broke into a melodramatic wail. "Please, sir! Please! Let me do one decent thing in my miserable life!"

"Fine! Goddamn, fine! Just quit your fucking blubbering!"

Falsch sniffled, trying not to smile. He'd taken the bait.

Tremaglio crouched down on one knee. Wesley stood behind him, still watching from behind his folded arms. Cera tried to shoot Falsch a meaningful look, knowing instinctively he was up to something, but he ignored her. His attention was focused fully on Tremaglio, who reached for Falsch's foot with his left hand. In his right, he still held his gun: the safety disengaged, finger beside the trigger guard, and the barrel pointed toward the ceiling.

Falsch had one chance to get this right. This time, should the unthinkable happen and he bungle the trick, there was no hidden loop to prevent the noose from tightening around his neck.

As soon as the Mafioso's fingers grazed his shoe, the magician attacked. With his right hand, he swung the loose handcuff at Tremaglio's nose like a morning star. With his left, he shook his arm to free the smoke bomb and threw it to the floor. The smoke bomb and Tremaglio's nose both cracked open at the same instant. Red blood and purple smoke burst out of their broken casings.

"Fuck!" Tremaglio stumbled backwards.

Wesley leapt into action, surging forward into the smoke to strangle Falsch. But the illusionist, having anticipated this, grabbed his chair and hurled it with all his strength at the shopkeeper's tattooed face.

The chair only bought him a couple seconds, maybe less, but still enough time for the smoke to swell and obfuscate the small, windowless room. By the time Tremaglio and Wesley had caught themselves, the smoke was thick enough to choke on. Falsch hit the ground, hiding below eye level where the purple clouds were the most impenetrable.

"You're dead!" Tremaglio spat. "You're fuckin' dead, you understand?!"

Falsch stretched his right thumb out of place, freeing his hand from the remaining cuff. He crawled on his belly beneath the smoke up behind Cera. "Thank God," she whispered. "Get me out of here."

Falsch didn't respond, pulling a hairpin out from behind her ear. He stuck the pin into his now-empty pair of handcuffs and worked it by feel until the cuffs popped open. He crawled away again, still leaving her cuffed in place. "Wait!" she hissed. "Where are you going? Get back here!"

He paid her no mind. Instead, he snuck up behind Tremaglio and Wesley and latched the newly opened handcuffs in place — one cuff around Tremaglio's left ankle, and the other around Wesley's right.

As soon as Tremaglio felt something graze his ankle, he swung his fist instinctively toward the sensation. His knuckles caught Falsch in the jaw.

The magician spat blood and teeth.

Tremaglio spun around with his gun to finish the job. Falsch leapt at him, grabbing for the gun with both hands.

Wesley tried to pull to the right, while Tremaglio pulled to the left. Neither went in the direction they intended to. Instead, Falsch's flying tackle sent them all to the floor.

As they hit the concrete, Tremaglio lost his grip and the gun went spinning across the floor, somewhere into the smoke. That would have to be good enough.

Falsch pushed himself upright and ran for the door. Tremaglio tried to grab for him, but Wesley tripped over the handcuffs as he tried to stand, pulling them both to the floor a second time.

Falsch made the stairs, taking them two at a time.

"Bobby!" Cera screamed, pulling against her handcuffs. "Bobby, you selfish bitch!"

Falsch paused as he reached the top of the stairs. He turned back and took a little bow.

"Ladies and gentlemen," he gloated, "the vanishing act!"

His ego satisfied, he disappeared through the door. On the other side, he found himself back behind the counter of the pawn shop. Falsch sprinted for the front door that led back onto the street. Despite his injuries, a satisfied smile illuminated his face. The greatest escape of his career — no, *of all time!* — and he was about to pull it off.

But just as he was about to wrap his fingers around the door handle, it opened from the other side. Falsch suddenly found himself face-to-face with a badge-wielding detective flanked by uniformed officers. Far from his favorite sight in the world, and certainly not one he was expecting at that moment. He almost couldn't believe it.

"Officers," Falsch began, "thank god you're here! I barely managed to escape—"

"On the ground!" One of the cops grabbed his arm and wrangled him down, shoving his face into the floor. For the third time that day, a pair of handcuffs clicked into place around his wrists.

"Wait, this is all a big misunderstanding," the magician cried. "I'm the victim here!"

"Yeah, yeah," the cop said. "Tell 'em down at the precinct."

The officer threw Falsch in the backseat of a cruiser. The cop car pulled away from the curb, carrying Falsch off to the nearest police station. The illusionist rested his throbbing head against the cool glass window, cursing his rotten luck.

●　●　●

The cops threw Falsch back in an interrogation room without letting him see a doctor. So much for the city of brotherly love.

Near as Falsch could figure, the police must've had Wild Wesley's staked out for some time. If the shop was laundering money for the Mafia — and all signs pointed in that direction — they must've been watching for weeks, maybe longer, slowly gathering enough evidence to get a warrant for the no-knock raid they enacted that night. And out of all the pawn shops in the city, out of all possible nights, Falsch had to pick that one, on that night, at that time. What were the odds?

Despite his circumstances, he retained a glimmer of hope. The cops had been there for Wesley, and they got him. They'd even picked up Tremaglio, a bigger fish than they probably expected to catch that night. As far as the cops should've been concerned, Falsch and Cera were just a couple of bystanders in the wrong place at the wrong time. He was simply a magician who had stopped in to browse the pawn shop's selection. Nothing criminal.

After more than two hours had elapsed, more than enough time for Falsch to practice his story in his head, the door finally opened. In stepped a detective, a different one than the one at the scene, with broad shoulders, an ill-fitting suit, and an oil black high-and-tight.

"Evening," the detective said, taking a seat opposite Falsch. "Name's Jameson."

"Evening, sir," Falsch said. "Can I see a doctor, please, before my statement? I'm in a great deal of pain…"

"Don't you worry," Detective Jameson winked. "This shouldn't take long. Your name?"

"Byron Davenport," Falsch said.

"Byron Davenport, huh?" Jameson asked. "That's your legal name?"

"Yes, sir."

Jameson smiled, revealing twin rows of crooked teeth. "Spell it for me."

Falsch did so.

"And can you tell me what your business was at Wild Wesley's Pawn Shop tonight?"

"Merely to peruse their offerings," Falsch said, in his best squeaky-clean voice. "I'd just finished a rather successful show, so I thought I might treat myself if I found something that tickled my fancy."

"What do you mean, finished a show?"

"I'm a magician, you see. They call me 'the bewitching' Byron Davenport."

"A magician?" The detective cocked an eyebrow. "Like sleight-of-hand?"

"Precisely, sir."

"Y'know, when you think about it..." Jameson placed a hand to his chin. "That ain't all so different from pickpocketing, is it?"

Falsch's heart skipped a beat, but he never broke his smile. "Not true at all, sir. The magician aims only to dazzle and inspire, not to steal."

"It's a lie though, ain't it? Magic. It's not real."

"...in a sense," Falsch conceded.

"So if you make your living lying to your audience, how is anyone supposed to trust you're not lying about other stuff?"

The conversation was not going as planned. Falsch didn't like the tone of Jameson's voice. It was smug, almost playful — like he knew something that Falsch didn't.

Falsch shifted in his seat. "Should I have a lawyer present?"

"Do you feel like you need one?"

Falsch didn't answer. A heavy quiet hung over the interrogation room for a long moment. When Jameson eventually broke the silence, he spoke slowly, as if relishing the taste of each syllable.

"You know, I just got finished talkin' with the women they picked up at the scene," he said. "Said she was your partner."

"Olga?"

"What'd you say her name was?"

Falsch desperately prayed Cera had given the cops the alias he'd used at the shop. "Olga Haberdasher?"

Jameson's smile grew wider. "Spell it for me."

Falsch did so.

"We had a very interesting conversation, 'Olga' and I," Jameson said. "In fact, she asked me to give you something."

"What's that?"

Jameson produced a folded post-it from his pocket and tossed it across the table. Falsch unfolded it with sweaty hands. Inside was a short note in Cera's handwriting.

"Where would a magician be without his fabulous assistant?"

Falsch remembered the answer he had given Cera earlier that evening, onstage at the Forrest Theatre before showtime.

"In my case? Probably in jail."

They'd both laughed at the time. It didn't seem so funny now.

Falsch's heart beat a frantic drumbeat against his ribcage. Before he could collect his thoughts, Jameson leaned in over the table, still smiling like a smug snake.

"Let me ask you a question, Bobby — I mean, 'Byron.'" The detective winked again. "You ever been to San Francisco?"

Cera had talked.

The color drained from Falsch's face. He stared at the detective, slack-jawed and wide-eyed. Jameson laughed, open-mouthed and full-throated.

"Oh, I love seein' criminals realize how fucked they are," the cop cackled. "That look on your face? Now *that's* real magic."

Falsch swallowed hard, suddenly crushed beneath the looming weight of an impending prison sentence.

"I think I'll take that lawyer now."

INQUIRE AT JOHNNY'S DINER

Ray loaded up an omelet with a blanket of cheese, mushrooms, onions, bell pepper, tomatoes and crumbled bacon before ever-so-gently wriggling his spatula beneath the ponderous mattress of fluffy yellow egg. The perfect omelet flip was a delicate dance, a precise balance of force and finesse. He flexed his fingers around the spatula handle like a gunslinger before a fast draw.

Ray stuck out his tongue and held it between his teeth. Hashbrowns and bacon sizzled on the grill. *The Good, the Bad and the Ugly* droned on a TV somewhere in the background. Two seconds ticked by on the clock above the door to the dining room. Ray's eyes narrowed. A single drop of sweat escaped the dollar store bandana holding back his greasy black hair.

Moment of truth.

He took a sharp breath inward, held it, and began the flip.

Simultaneously, the dining room door burst open and Johnny exploded into the kitchen. "Ray, I've got *neeeeews!* I've got huge news!"

Ray jerked, sending the omelet splattering into a dozen pieces that sizzled across the flattop. He sighed.

"Don't even worry about it," Johnny said.

"Johnny, we got like seven tickets up."

"And you have a customer!"

"We have lots of customers! Like the one at table eight," Ray continued, already cracking more eggs, "who's going to be waiting for another omelet."

"Which *I'll* make," Johnny insisted, "because *you* have a customer."

"Wait, you mean, like, my thing?"

Johnny gave an earnest nod, his bright red hair flopping like a puppy's ears. "Yeah, dude! The Reynolds Detective Agency's first real client."

"Oh *shit…!*"

Ray peered out the porthole in the kitchen door into the dining room. Seated on the peeling vinyl of the backmost corner booth and nursing a black coffee was a figure Ray recognized — a thin, wiry man with silver glasses and chestnut hair, only a few years older than him, but wearing a suit that Ray could neither afford nor pull off.

Ray took off his gloves and dabbed sweat from his face using his apron.

"Okay, how do I look? Professional?"

Johnny gave him a once-over, taking in the grease splatters and unevenly trimmed facial hair speckled with gray. "Totally." He gave Ray a thumbs up. "Looking good."

Ray took a deep breath, smacked himself in the face a couple times to get the blood going, and slunk out into the dining room.

"Well, well, well," Ray said, sliding into the booth. "Good to see you, Franklin baby. How you been?"

The suited man — one Franklin Conway, a local attorney — affixed Ray with a dubious stare, one eyebrow raised above the wire frames of his glasses. "Mr. Reynolds. Charming as ever."

He slid a cheaply printed business card across the table. "REYNOLDS DETECTIVE AGENCY," it read. "GOOD INVESTIGATIONS, DONE CHEAP. Inquire at Johnny's Diner." The attorney tapped a little hole poked in one corner of the card.

"I found that pinned into the corkboard at Rutter's. Is this your idea of building a client base?"

Ray grinned. "Got *you* here, didn't it?"

Conway sighed, leaning back in the booth. "You are a deeply unserious person, aren't you, Mr. Reynolds?"

"I figure you're serious enough for the both of us." He shrugged. "World's filled up with serious people. What do we need another one for?"

The lawyer smiled. "You know, Mr. Reynolds, in spite of everything, I've always liked you. You did some fine reporting." He sipped his coffee. "Damn shame about the paper."

"Thanks, I appreci— wait, what do you mean, 'in spite of everything?'"

Conway chuckled. "Let's get down to brass tacks, shall we? My firm is handling a case for which we require the services of a private investigator. I've convinced my partner to take a chance on you, instead of the agency from the next county over we typically retain."

"Aw shucks," Ray placed a hand over his heart. "You believe in me that much?"

"You're local. Means we pay out less for mileage."

"Practical as ever, I see."

"It's a simple matter. Even you should be able to handle it."

"*Even* me, huh? Golly gee."

Conway glanced over his shoulder, then leaned in conspiratorially. "It's a standard workers' compensation case. An employee of our client is claiming a workplace injury that he alleges leaves him unable to work. We have our doubts. You merely need to observe, document, and report back. We would be highly interested in any behavior inconsistent with his alleged injury."

Ray shrugged. "Seems doable."

"I should hope so. What's your fee? I believe there was some mention of 'cheap?'"

Ray winced, wishing he'd listened to Johnny's advice to come up with a different tagline. Or that he'd gotten around to coming up with a price sheet.

Ray threw out a number, higher than he expected the attorney to accept.

"Plus expenses?" the attorney offered, helpfully.

"Shit! Yeah, plus expenses."

"Done."

Ray did a little fist pump. Conway rubbed his temples in exasperated circles.

"I'll have my secretary send you over…" The attorney trailed off, looking around the diner. "You… don't have a printer, do you?"

"No, but we got this fancy Belgian waffle maker that Johnny insisted on buying."

"Heaven help me." Conway took a final sip of his coffee and stood to leave. "Stop by the office when you get out of here. We'll have a file and a contract for you." He turned to leave, but looked back. "And a final word of advice? Get yourself a proper office somewhere. You need to inspire *confidence* in your clients, not…" He waved a hand up and down at Ray's person. "Whatever this is."

"Cool, unsolicited advice. My favorite. Thanks, man."

"Consider yourself lucky. My advice is typically solicited at great cost."

Ray watched Conway leave, wondering if he could cram a desk and chair into the broom closet. He stood and moseyed back to the kitchen, passing by table eight on the way. The patron sat drumming their fingers against the empty table.

"Johnny, we're still waiting on that omelet!"

• • •

Ray stuck around through the lunch rush. Waffles and omelets turned to club sandwiches and burgers. "So you're stalking some injured guy?" Johnny asked while Ray was cleaning up, getting ready to go.

"Not stalking, dude. *Surveilling*. Wanna come, be my deputy?"

Johnny shook his head. "Sorry man. After closing this place down, Troy's finally back in town. Date night!"

"That sounds nice… What're y'all doing?"

"I dunno. Maybe see what's playing out at the drive-in. Maybe lie under the stars, smoke a joint. Maybe just make out in his truck somewhere."

"Goddamn, that sounds way more fun than my thing."

"Sucks to be you!"

Ray laughed. "Yeah, usually does."

He drove over to Conway's law firm, an office housed in a converted rancher on Matilda Avenue. The woman at the front desk sniffed the air when he entered. "You smell like bacon," she informed him.

"Is that a bad thing?"

"It's better than what you usually smell like."

Ray leaned in on the desk. "I've actually really cut back, for the record."

"I'm sure you have," she said, producing a file folder from her desk.

Ray slapped his signature on the contract and left. He read through the paperwork in his Bronco out in the parking lot. The subject's name was Edward Munsen, of 425 Phillips Street, an employee of Detweiler Landscaping. He'd told his bosses he'd busted up his knee unloading equipment at a job site, leaving him hobbling around and hardly fit for work. Seemed pretty cut and dry to Ray. Either he was faking or he wasn't.

He stopped by home, where he permitted himself a single hit off his weed pen. And then another. And then a third, just for good measure. His head pleasantly abuzz, Ray hopped in the shower to rinse of the smell of bacon. Satisfied that he smelled like Irish Spring instead of salty grease, he threw on a Johnny Cash shirt, a faded flannel, and his battered old flat-top Stetson hat. He grabbed his camera — a Nikon he'd liberated from the newsroom when the paper shuttered — and drove across town.

The little yellow house sat on an unkempt lawn inside a rusting waist-high chain link fence. Ray parked across the street and tried to look inconspicuous, a difficult task when you're loitering in a car taking pictures through somebody's window. Any time a child rode by on a bike, or a couple walked by with a dog, Ray scrooched down in his seat like a creeper, hiding his camera beneath his hat.

Through the window, Ray could see Munsen on his couch, both feet propped up. A thickly built bear of a man, he sat watching Fox News and nursing a beer. A bag of frozen peas rested overtop his left knee. For the first hour, the most he moved was to lift an ass cheek and scratch. Nothing that would strain his supposedly injured knee. Eventually, when he did lift himself to fetch a fresh beer and a new bag of frozen veggies, Ray noticed a pronounced limp as he dragged himself out of view. Seemed real enough to Ray. He snapped a sequence of photos as evidence.

Poor Franklin's sure gonna be disappointed…

Not like it mattered to Ray. He got paid just as much if Munsen was telling the truth as he would if he were faking. Over the second hour, Ray tailed him down to Rutter's, where he bought a bundle of scratch-offs and powerball tickets, but he limped the whole time. Back at home, Munsen took a quarter to the scratch-offs. By the way he broke a beer bottle against the wall, Ray figured they were losers. Munsen didn't bother cleaning up the broken glass, just grabbed another beer and limped back to his couch.

How long am I 'sposed to watch him for?

After the third hour, Ray's attention had started to flag. The early autumn sun began to enter the golden hour as Ray's lids drooped lazily in front of his eyes. *Wasn't being a PI supposed to be… exciting?*

He'd almost slipped into an involuntary nap, right there in his seat, when the sound of a slamming car door jerked him back to attention. Across the street, a gleaming black Firebird had rolled to a stop in front of Munsen's house. Two figures emerged from the car, one sporting a long blonde mullet and a pair of brass knuckles, the other with a shaved head and a length of steel pipe. Both wore denim vests with matching patches that dominated their backs: a screaming bald eagle, wrapped in a red, white, and blue banner, with the letters S. O. E. beneath. Whatever they were there for, it sure as shit wasn't selling candy bars for the school fundraiser.

Ray watched the scene unfold through his camera lens, peeking above the edge of his window with his camera like an infantryman in a foxhole, capturing the entire proceeding.

The two intruders kicked in the cheap plywood door like wet tissue paper. Munsen tried to run, but his injured knee seemed more genuine than ever. The redneck with the pipe smashed the metal club into his already-busted knee before he could escape, sending him crashing to the floor. The other one stood overtop, hollering something in his face. Munsen said something back, but it must've not been the answer they were looking for, because he cracked the metal knuckles across his jaw. Munsen dropped like a sack of potatoes, out cold.

Without a second thought, the redneck with the mullet and the knuckles hoisted Munsen up over his shoulder and carried the unconscious man out of the house toward the idling sports car. Ray ducked down in his seat, heartbeat pounding in his ears. He peeked out again at the sound of the motor roaring and caught sight of the Firebird burning rubber down the quiet street, carrying Munsen off to parts unknown.

Ray blinked and the car was gone. The whole thing had taken less than a minute.

"What," Ray rubbed his eyes, "the fuck just happened?"

• • •

This was bigger than a worker's comp case. Edward Munsen had gotten himself into some kind of shit, and it looked like it fell to ole Ray to try to get him out of it.

Goddamn it… Always some fuckin' bullshit…

Ray sped over to the courthouse. He made it with five minutes before to spare, and was up the stairs to the District Attorney's office with two minutes left on the clock before the end of the day. He burst into the DA's suite like Kramer into Jerry's apartment in an episode of Seinfeld, yelling: "Owen!"

Owen Engels looked up from behind her desk, situated inside a private office at the far end of the suite. The sight of her — soft, straw-colored hair cropped above her shoulders, accentuated by the sharp angles of her black pantsuit — was still enough to put a lump in Ray's throat. The sight of Ray bounding toward her, conversely, was enough to send Owen's eyes rolling to the back of her head. She emitted a mighty sigh. "Heaven help me…"

"Owen!" Ray reached her office and took the liberty of closing the door behind him. "Owen, I have *good* news and *terrible* news."

"Ray, this isn't the salon at Wal-Mart. We don't take walk-ins."

"The good news," Ray said anyway, "is that I got my first case."

"Had to happen eventually, I suppose…"

"The terrible news is he's been kidnapped."

Now she took interest. "Who has?"

"I can't say," Ray said.

"What do you mean, you can't say?"

"Client… detective… privilege…?"

Ray hadn't had the opportunity to use that one yet. He hoped he was using it right.

Owen shook her head. "So let me get this straight…" Ray winced. It was never good when she started with that. "You burst into my office, at 4:58, *on a Friday,* to tell me about something you *refuse to actually tell me about?*"

"Um…"

"Look, Ray," Owen sighed. "I'm a busy woman. If you have knowledge of a crime, call the police. That's how that works. Don't come kicking in my door."

"Alright, listen, *hypothetically,* I may have been retained to surveil *someone,* for *reasons.* And that someone, *theoretically,* may have been grabbed by a couple shitkickers in a vintage Firebird, with *this* back patch on their vests."

Ray showed her one of the photos, zoomed in to display only the eagle patch. Owen raised an eyebrow.

"Hypothetically?" she asked.

Ray nodded eagerly.

"Hypothetically, you *still* need to file a report. I'll get the station on the line right now."

She reached for her desk phone. Ray lurched forward and held her hand down to prevent her from picking it up. Owen glared at his hand. Blood began to color her cheeks red. Ray knew her well enough to know it wasn't from embarrassment.

"Look, this is my first case, and I really need to prove myself, okay? All I'm asking for is a little time. Then, if I don't have it resolved, I'll report it. One day. Twenty-four hours. That's it. Please?"

Owen yanked her hand out. "I'll give you *three*."

"Days?!"

Plenty of time!

"No, dipshit," Owen said. "Three *hours*, and you're lucky I'm even giving you that."

Oh. Shit.

She pointed to his camera. "Do you know who you're dealing with?"

Ray flashed his most ingratiating grin. "I was hoping you could tell me?"

"The Sons of Eagles, they call themselves. Real patriotic. Led by a guy they call Lethal Lester. Fancy themselves a proper gang, but they're more like a bunch of methed-up cousin fuckers."

"What do they do?"

"Oh, the usual for their type. Smoke meth. Sell meth. Rough folks up for money. Mostly, they get drunk at their 'base of operations,' a biker bar and grill out past Lawnsdale."

"What's it called?"

"If I tell you, what're you gonna do?"

Ray blinked. "Wha?"

She leaned in over the desk. "What are you gonna *do* with this information? You're not dumb enough to just waltz in the front door, are you?"

"I'm not going to do *anything*, Owen. This whole conversation has been *hypothetical*, remember?"

A smile tugged at the corner of her mouth. "Good. The place is called The Steel Horse."

"Awesome," Ray smiled. "Thank you, Owen!"

"You really want to thank me?"

Ray nodded enthusiastically.

"Then *get the hell out of my office.*"

He couldn't help but laugh. Same old Owen.

"Remember," she called after him on his way out, "Three hours!"

• • •

Even with a quick stop back home to grab his food-splattered apron, Ray was outside The Steel Horse in just over thirty minutes. The place was a converted Victorian house fallen into disrepair, located on a hill surrounded by trees with leaves painted autumnal reds, yellows and oranges. A single lane led up the hill to the bar. One way in, one way out. Ray didn't like that.

Beside the hill, next to the highway, a Dollar General and a butcher shop enticed passersby from a pothole-spotted parking lot. He left his Bronco behind the two shops, tucked safely out of sight, and climbed up the backside of the hill. Draped in his apron, Ray emerged from the treeline behind the bar like a feral line cook raised by wolves. The back door stood propped up by a can of baked beans. Ray took a quick lap around the perimeter. Out in front, a line of Harleys stood at attention. Beside them, the Firebird gleamed in the fading sunlight.

They're here, alright.

Of course Ray wasn't going to just waltz in the front door. He didn't know how to waltz, and despite all indications to the contrary, he wasn't actually an idiot. He was going to make a distraction out front and then sneak in the *back,* through the kitchen. Hopefully he could be in and out before anybody realized he wasn't just another grungy cook.

He stepped up to the line of bikes.

People have been fuckin' killed for what I'm about to do.

Ray took a deep breath.

Then he gave the nearest Harley a heavy shove, sending it careening into the motorcycle next to it, setting off a chain of elaborate, expensive dominoes. The sound of crashing metal erupted like cannon fire.

Jesus Christ, maybe I am an idiot…

Ray ran around the back as leather-clad tough guys came hollering out the front door. He slipped through the propped-open door like a cat and slinked quietly through the dirty chrome kitchen. The cooks had abandoned their posts to watch the chaos unfolding out in the dining room. The patrons furiously accused one another of not properly securing their bikes. Ray noticed the two rednecks from before, with the mullet and the shaved head, observing impassively, not buying into the mounting rage between the drunk bikers.

He needed to move quickly.

Ray knew that if they'd brought Munsen here, he wouldn't be out front in the dining room. And he wouldn't be in the kitchen. He would be somewhere out of the way, where he couldn't make trouble. In the back of the kitchen, behind a closed door, he found a set of stairs leading down to the basement. Ray descended into the depths of the house.

Shelf-stable ingredients stood at attention around the basement: canned meats and veggies, bags of burger and hot dog buns, seasonings and unopened condiments. Set into one wall, a heavy chrome door sealed off the walk-in from the rest of the room. From beyond it, Ray could make out a thumping noise. And then a muted voice: "Let me out! Please! I don't have the money, but I'll get it, I swear!"

Ray glanced behind him to make sure nobody was coming down the stairs before rushing to the door. He pulled open the heavy metal slab. Inside, stripped down to only a pair of ratty boxers, shivered Edward Munsen.

"I swear to god I'll get the money," he said through chattering teeth. "I just need a little more time, okay?"

"I'm not with them," Ray said, grabbing him by the arm.

"Then who the hell are you?"

"The guy who's getting you out of here," he answered, yanking him out of the walk-in.

Munsen made it two steps before collapsing, yowling in pain and clutching his knee.

"Shush up," Ray hissed, slipping his arm under Munsen's shoulders. "You want them to hear us?"

Ray was a little guy, smaller than Munsen by at least half a foot. By the time he'd dragged Munsen up the stairs, Ray was huffing and puffing like he'd run a marathon. At the top, he put a finger to his lips at Munsen and slowly cracked the door to check if the coast was clear.

"Well, well," said the mullet-haired shitkicker on the other side. "What do we have here?"

Mullet Man ripped the door the rest of the way open, fully revealing Ray with his arm wrapped around Munsen. The shaven-head slab of muscle stood beside his friend, both of them wearing ugly smiles.

"Oh fuck," Munsen muttered.

"Hey fellas," Ray smiled, feigning nonchalance. "I was just grabbing some chicken from the walk-in, and, uh…" He trailed off, unsure how to land that particular plane.

"Now Willy, do you remember the boss hiring a new cook?" asked the one with the mullet.

"Now Billy," answered smooth-shaven Willy, "I can't say that I do."

"Well then…" Billy lifted his foot and planted a size-twelve boot into Ray's chest hard enough to send them both tumbling down the stairs.

Ray cracked his face against the bottom step and came to lay face-up, stars swirling around the edges of his vision. Munsen landed beside him, moaning in agony. A pair of arms wrapped themselves under Ray's arms, dragging him along the floor.

"Take your stinking paws off me, you damn dirty ape!"

A set of knuckles across the jaw sent him to unconsciousness.

• • •

The cold woke him up. Ray dragged himself upright on the walk-in floor, groaning. At least they hadn't taken his clothes, like they did Munsen's.

"'Bout time."

"Wha?"

"A-bout fuck-in' time," Munsen grunted. He was huddled up in one corner, flab jiggling and teeth chattering like a misfiring metronome.

"How long was I out?" Ray rubbed his hand along his jaw.

"Do I look like I'm wearing a watch? Long enough that it can't be good for you."

"Great…"

Ray patted himself down. The idiots hadn't taken his phone, but he only had one bar. He called Johnny. The dial tone sounded like it was coming through a string and a tin can.

"Come on… come on…"

"Who are you calling?"

Ray glanced at him. "Call it the cavalry."

It went to voicemail. "*Heeeeere's* Johnny! You know how this works."

"Shit!"

"What is it?" Munsen asked.

"It's date night!"

"*What?*"

"It's fucking date night!" Ray repeated, as if that explained it. The voicemail beeped. "Listen Johnny, SOS! I repeat, full-blown SOS fuckin' emergency, we're at The Steel Horse, outside Lawnsdale, locked downstairs in the—"

His phone chirped, interrupting to tell him it had dropped the call. His single bar of service had vanished. Ray resisted the urge to smash the damned thing into the walk-in floor. Munsen's teeth clacked together so loudly the sound echoed around the frosty metal chamber.

"Jesus fucking Christ, here, man…" Ray removed his flannel overshirt.

Munsen snatched it from his hands and desperately wrapped it around himself. "So… who exactly the fuck *are* you?"

Ray took a moment. This is what he came up with: "Um, my name's Ray…"

Munsen blinked. "Okay? *Why the fuck are you here?*"

Ray took another moment. This time he came up with something better. "The truth is… I'm a private detective." Panic came over Munsen's face, but Ray had an angle. "See, I've been working with the Detweiler County district attorney looking into this gang, the Sons of Eagles. More like sons of bitches, am I right?"

Munsen still seemed apprehensive. "So why're you springing me? How'd you know I was here?"

Ray nodded for several straight seconds to buy some time.

"I was… tailing Willy and Billy, gathering intel. Right? Next thing I know, they're kicking in your door and hauling you away. I figure you can help us nail these bastards. That's why I need you to tell me everything you know about these boys, on the record, to help me put 'em up in the state pen for the next ten to twenty."

Ray opened the recording app on his phone. The sight of it made Munsen go skittish again: "I ain't done *nothin'* and I don't know *nothin'* and I ain't sayin' *nothin'*."

Ray took another approach, adopting the comforting tone his therapist used with him when he got overwhelmed with things.

"I'm on *your* side here, buddy. Okay? All we're interested in is putting these bastards away. Whatever you've done to get yourself here, we don't care. We're talkin' immunity. We just need the truth — all of it — so we can stick it to these Sons of Eagles."

Munsen eyed him up, considering it.

Ray almost had him.

"You promise?" Munsen asked.

"Scout's Honor," Ray said, doing the salute wrong. He'd never been a scout.

Neither had Munsen, apparently. "Well the first thing you have to understand is, it weren't my fault."

Ray tapped record on his phone. "Private detective Ray Reynolds here, confirming this conversation is being recorded as part of an ongoing investigation." Munsen looked like he wanted to retreat back into his shell, but Ray smiled encouragingly. "So whose fault is it?"

"My whore of an ex-wife," Munsen spat, sexist anger supplanting his apprehension.

Ray nodded. "*Women,* right?" It was gross, but he needed to lean into it. Make Munsen feel he could open up. "What's her name?"

"Tabitha Munsen," he said. "At least until the paperwork goes through."

Ray smiled. By giving his ex-wife's name, Ray'd gotten him to inadvertently confirm his own identity without having to ask directly.

Munsen continued bitching. "She leaves *me,* says *I'm* the problem, then only a month later, she's choking on some other dick?" He growled like a dog. "After everything I done for her? I don't fucking think so."

"How'd you know?"

"Saw 'em."

"Saw 'em where?"

"Wherever they went."

"Followed 'em?"

"You know how it is," Munsen shrugged. "Gotta keep an eye on what's yours."

Internally Ray retched, but outwardly he nodded quietly, employing the old reporter's trick of letting the silence invite Munsen to keep speaking.

"She always knew just how to work me up," Munsen continued, working himself up just fine without any help. "What buttons to press to make me see red. So when I saw her with her new boytoy, I just… I just…" He sputtered, too angry to form the words.

"Started seeing red?"

"Exactly. So… maybe I hear about these fellas…"

"The Sons of Eagles?"

Munsen nodded. "And, yeah, maybe I think they can help me with my little problem."

"Uh-huh."

"So maybe I ask 'em to put the fear of god into the new boyfriend. Give him a few new bruises if he's braver than he looks. Whatever it takes to scare him off, show Tabby how it feels when someone walks out on you. Would serve the bitch right."

"And you couldn't pay?"

"I paid up front, but the fuckers upped the price afterward. Came back and said he'd required a strong hand. Said I owed 'em double!"

Ray nodded. "The bastards."

"The bastards! I tell 'em I only had what we agreed to, and you know what the fuckers do? Take a steel pipe to my fucking knee!"

There it is. Ding. Ding. Ding. Jackpot!

Munsen was on a roll now. "Now let me ask you a question. How do you figure I'm supposed to get their goddamn money if I got a busted knee and can't fuckin' *work*?"

"I don't rightly know," Ray said thoughtfully. "Outside of sellin' drugs? 'Bout the only thing that comes to mind is…" *Don't overplay it.* "…maybe try to play it as a workplace injury, get them to pay for it?"

Munsen clapped his hands together. Ray jumped.

Did I blow it?

"That's exactly what *I* thought! Thought myself pretty clever, but guess what?"

Ray breathed a small sigh of relief. "What?"

"Turns out, anything like that has to go through workers' comp, and workers' comp only pays *part* of your regular wage! So now I'm making even less, my knee's all fucked up, can't work, can't pay 'em off… They said they'd give me a month. 'Stead, they came back in two weeks." He shrugged. "Now I'm here."

Ray nodded, finally seeing the completed puzzle.

Franklin oughta like this. Assuming we make it out of here…

"So…" Musen rubbed himself, hopelessly trying to get warm. "When's your cavalry comin' to get us?"

That was an excellent question. Ray couldn't even be sure Johnny had gotten the message. Fortunately, or not-so-fortunately, they were interrupted before Ray had to answer. The walk-in door opened; Ray shoved away his phone. Billy, Willy, and a new figure stood on the other side. The newcomer stood decked in leather and metal studs, a head taller than both his enforcers. He looked like he'd taken a bad slide across the asphalt without a helmet at some point, half his face dominated by gnarled scars.

"This is them," Billy sneered. "We caught the short one breaking in, trying to rescue ole Eddie here."

"Slit his belly, boss! Son-of-a-bitch knocked over the *bikes*."

Lethal Lester grabbed Ray by the collar and lifted him as easily as lifting a toddler. He held him close to his mottled face, close enough Ray could taste the stink of his breath.

"Look mister," Ray squeaked, "this is all just some big misunderstanding. I'm just a line cook!"

He headbutted Ray between the eyes for his trouble. The force of the blow momentarily forced his spirit from his body. When he came to again, he was on the basement floor and Munsen had been dragged out next to him. Billy and Willy were taking turns sinking their boots into his belly, demanding the money he owed.

"I'll get it!" Munsen moaned, begging. "Please! Please, stop!"

Lester loomed down over Ray. "You like it?" He tapped his forehead, revealing the solid thunk of a metal plate. "The one good thing that came out of my accident."

Ray groaned, his head still spinning. "You mean you don't like looking like a Batman villain?"

The gang leader slapped the back of his hand across Ray's mouth. "Don't insult an accident survivor's looks. Ain't your momma teach you better than that?"

Ray spat a little blood. "Okay, you know what, that's fair… Sorry for that one…"

Lester smiled. "Looks like you can be taught manners. That's good. That's a start." He snapped his fingers at Billy and Willy. "You two. Pliers. Battery. Cables. Fetch." The two mooks sprung to action like well-trained dogs, disappearing back up the stairs. He turned back to Ray and Munsen, smiling with a mouthful of rotten teeth. "I think you two are about to have a little accident of your own." He let his hands come to rest on his hips, drawing attention to the Smith & Wesson revolver tucked into his waistband.

Munsen gulped. Ray was inclined to agree with him.

The door at the top of the stairs opened again. But instead of Billy and Willy returning with their torture devices, it was one of the cooks. "Um… boss?"

Lester shot him a venomous glare. "I said no interruptions."

"I know, but truck's here, and this new delivery guy is being a real bitch and demanding to see the owner."

Ray's breath caught in his throat. *Johnny!*

Sure enough, Johnny's tenor sounded from upstairs: "Out of the way, gotta see whoever's in charge. Supply chains are *fucked* right now. Hey, move it, let me through. You know what they say about breaking eggs?" He pushed the cook out of the way, emerging down the stairs carrying a cardboard box full of egg cartons.

While everyone was distracted, Ray shifted his weight, preparing to move.

"What the hell," Lester hollered, his hand moving to his revolver. "Somebody get him outta here!"

But before anyone could follow out the order, Johnny hurled the box directly at his face. The box hit him in the nose with a dull, heavy thud, knocking him to the ground. The eggs came spilling out across the floor, cracking open and sending little rivulets of broken yellow yolk spreading throughout the basement.

"Looks like we just made an omelet," Johnny said. He blew imaginary smoke away from a pair of finger guns.

Ray used the opportunity to scramble to his feet and stumble forward, still disoriented. Lester was already pulling himself back up. Ray fixed that with a cowboy boot to the balls, as hard as he could. And then another. And then a third, just for good measure. While Lester howled in a newfound soprano, Ray yoinked the pistol from his pants, made sure the safety was on, and pulled Munsen to his feet.

"They worked me over pretty good…" he coughed.

Ray took him under one shoulder, Johnny under the other. They dragged him up the stairs like they were running a six-legged race.

"What'd you think of my omelet line?" Johnny asked.

"Four out of ten on the pun," Ray huffed, "but perfect marks on the timing."

The kitchen staff stayed out of their way, hands raised. Ray waved the gun around anyway, for dramatic effect. Willy and Billy entered from outside, carrying the jumper cables, car battery and pliers. "What the hell's going on in…" Billy trailed off at the sight of the revolver in Ray's hand, but the two rednecks held their ground, blocking the exit.

"Looks like we got ourselves an old-fashioned standoff," Ray said.

"Doodle-loodle-doo! *Wahh wahh wahhhh*," Johnny said, imitating the music from *The Good, the Bad and the Ugly*. Munsen's eyes darted back and forth between their side and their opposition like the characters in the movie.

"Ain't too late to change your mind 'fore you really get hurt," Billy growled.

"You boys really wanna play battery, pliers, gun?" Ray laughed. "It's like rock, paper, scissors, except gun always wins."

The two mooks shared a sidelong glance. After a moment's deliberation, they moved out of the way. Ray tipped his hat as they left.

Johnny's boyfriend Troy, a heavyset guy with a reserved demeanor and neatly trimmed beard, sat idling in his semi-trailer in the parking lot, ready to make their getaway. He fidgeted with a trans pride keychain dangling from his rearview, a little flag with a white stripe between two soft pink stripes and two baby blue stripes.

"Y'all okay?" he asked, helping pull everyone up into the cab. "Did you use the omelet line?"

"I did," Johnny huffed, "and Ray only gave it a four!"

The engine rumbled and Troy pulled the truck out of the lot. Ray wiped away his prints and tossed the gun out the window on their way out. Lethal Lester stumbled out of the front door in time to see them make the main road, disappearing into traffic.

"Jesus Christ," Munsen groaned as they rolled down the road, still only in his boxers and Ray's flannel. "What a day."

Ray's phone started to ring, finally back in service. "Uh… hello?"

"It's been three hours," said Owen's voice. "How's your little problem?"

"Owen, what are you talking about?"

"You know damn well what I'm talking about."

"That whole conversation was *hypothetical*. Remember?"

"Of course. My bad. Night, Ray."

"Night, Owen… and, um, thank you."

A soft laugh. "Don't do it again." She hung up.

Johnny rested his head on Troy's shoulder, smiling up at his man. Ray admired their bliss. "Sorry for running y'all's date night," he said sheepishly.

"It's okay," Troy said. "Johnny always tells me about all the crazy shit you two get up to. It's kind of fun getting to be part of it this time."

He pecked Johnny on the top of the head.

"Besides," Johnny said, "I have an idea how you can make it up to us."

"Woah, woah, woah," Munsen protested, "hold on a second."

Ray looked at him. "What?"

Munsen looked back and forth between Johnny and Troy, a repulsed look on his face. "You didn't tell me the cavalry was a couple of faggots."

Johnny gasped. Troy's eyebrows shot up to the top of his forehead.

"Are you fuckin' *serious* right now, dude?" Ray snapped. "These guys just— You know what? No. We're done. Troy, pull over."

"You sure?"

"Completely. Fuck this guy."

Troy put on his blinker and pulled onto the shoulder.

"Wait, wait, wait," Munsen backtracked, "I didn't mean it. You can't toss me out here. The Sons of Eagles, they'll—"

"Not my fucking problem," Ray said. He reached past Munsen, opened his door, and shoulder-checked him out of the truck. He landed hard, flat on his ass.

"Hold on, wait! Please!"

"You can keep the shirt." Ray leaned out the window. "Oh, and by the way, I would expect to hear from a Mr. Franklin Conway about that workers' comp case of yours…"

They drove away, laughing at the dumbfounded look on his face.

● ● ●

Franklin Conway was just sitting down to dinner when the doorbell rang. His wife gave him an inquisitive look. He found Ray on his doorstep, face covered in new bruises.

"Good lord," Conway said. "You look like fresh hell."

"Yeah, I get that a lot."

"How do you know where I live?"

Ray gave him the *'are you an idiot?'* look people were always giving him. "I'm a *detective*, man."

Conway smiled slightly. "I suppose you are."

"You were wrong and you were right," Ray said. "It wasn't a simple matter. But I did handle it."

"Look Reynolds, I have dinner waiting. Do we have to do this now?"

Ray pressed play on his phone.

"'I paid up front, but the fuckers upped the price afterward. Came back and said he'd required a strong hand. Said I owed 'em double!' 'The bastards.' 'The bastards! I tell 'em I only had what we agreed to, and you know what the fuckers do? Take a steel pipe to my fucking knee!'"

Conway's brow furrowed. "What am I listening to?"

"Oh, just Edward Munsen admitting on tape — with his consent — that a biker gang smashed his knee in, not a workplace injury." Conway's eyebrows rose above the rims of his wire-framed glasses. "Not to mention the whole thing about stalking his ex-wife and hiring criminals to beat up her new boyfriend…"

"He *what?*"

Ray played the audio again. Conway's jaw dropped.

"This is phenomenal," the attorney said.

"Was hoping you'd say that."

Ray handed him an invoice, hand-written on a piece of scrap paper. The lawyer took it, examining the charges. He raised an eyebrow.

"How on earth did you have *fifteen dozen eggs* as an expense?"

Ray smiled. "Don't question my methods. But if you want to drop off the check at my office tomorrow, I'd be happy to tell you the whole story over a cup of joe."

"So you took my advice about the office. Where?"

"Inquire at Johnny's Diner," Ray shouted over his shoulder, already walking away.

• • •

Ray loaded up a pair of omelets with two blankets of cheese, mushrooms, onions, bell pepper, tomatoes and crumbled bacon before ever-so-gently wriggling his spatula beneath the first ponderous mattress of fluffy yellow egg. Hashbrowns and bacon sizzled in the background.

Out in the dining room, closed to the public this late, Johnny and Troy held hands across one of the tabletops, talking about everything and nothing while making goo-goo eyes at each other, finally enjoying their date night.

Ray stuck out his tongue and held it between his teeth. Two seconds ticked by on the clock above the door to the dining room. A single drop of sweat escaped the dollar store bandana holding back his greasy black hair.

He took a sharp breath inward, held it, and began the flip.

The omelet somersaulted with the grace of a trained gymnast and landed on its other side, all of its toppings still inside.

He repeated the action with the second omelet and stuck the landing.

Ray smiled to himself, whistling as he worked.

ACKNOWLEDGMENTS

This book appears with extreme gratitude to the following:

- My wife, Crystal, my first reader for everything I write, my biggest cheerleader, my toughest editor, and the love of my life.
- My mentor T. Fox Dunham, who over the years of our friendship has taught me more about writing and about life than I realized I still needed to learn.
- My dear friend Mary Siniscalchi, a wonderful artist whose talent I am honored to have grace the cover of this book, and whose friendship is a source of great joy.
- My family, including my kids Madi and London, my wife and I's co-parents in our beautiful blended family Clint and Bethany, my sister Cynthia, and my mom and dad, for their continued belief and support.
- Ron Earl Phillips and Shotgun Honey, for continuing to believe in my work and put up with me.
- Mark Westmoreland, for editing the collection in which this book's title story initially appeared, an important step in my journey and the development of my character Ray.

- And all my friends, especially Ashley and Francisco, whom I continually force to listen to me brainstorm, brag, and complain.

With gratitude, the following stories previously appeared in the following places.

- Born a Ramblin' Man (Trouble No More, Down & Out Books)
- My Heroes Have Already Been Cowboys (Red Headed Writing, Cowboy Jamboree Press)
- Railroad Blues (Shotgun Honey, as "Transcendent Ramblin' Railroad Blues")
- Once I Was Stoned (Hank Mighta Done It This Way, Cowboy Jamboree Press)
- …And Satan Came With Them (Blood and Blasphemy, HellBound Books)
- Down to the Knuckle (Close to the Bone Publishing)
- Wolf in Wolf's Clothing (Nightside: Tales of Outré Noir, Close to the Bone Publishing)
- Real Magic (Born Under a Bad Sign, Screaming Eye Press)

ABOUT THE AUTHOR

Michel Lee Garrett is an author, editor, Pennsyltucky poet, and recovering journalist. She has investigated courthouse corruption as a small-town reporter, directed communications for a U.S. Senate campaign, and served as the presidential speechwriter for a major research university. She is the author of "Born a Ramblin' Man" and the editor of "Burning Down The House: Crime Fiction Incited by the Songs of the Talking Heads," both available from Shotgun Honey, as well as the editor of "Transcendent Love: True Stories of Trans-for-Trans Relationships," forthcoming from Jessica Kingsley Publishers. A queer and trans writer, she is also an organizer and advocate for LGBT+ rights. She lives in Central Pennsylvania with her wife and two children. She has no free time. Find her online at LeeGarrett.net.

SHOTGUN HONEY BOOKS

Thank you for reading Born a Ramblin' Man by Michel Lee Garrett.

Shotgun Honey began as a crime genre flash fiction webzine in 2011 created as a venue for new and established writers to experiment in the confines of a mere 700 words. More than a decade later, Shotgun Honey still challenges writers with that storytelling task, but also provides opportunities to expand beyond through our book imprint and has since published anthologies, collections, novellas and novels by new and emerging authors.

We hope you have enjoyed this book. That you will share your experience, review and rate this title positively on your favorite book review sites and with your social media family and friends.

Visit ShotgunHoneyBooks.com

SHOTGUN HONEY
FICTION WITH A KICK